MARY M[...] [...]S

A

# AT HOME

## Charlotte Bingham

BANTAM BOOKS
TORONTO • NEW YORK • LONDON • SYDNEY • AUCKLAND

AT HOME
A BANTAM BOOK 0 553 40429 6

Originally published in Great Britain by
Michael Joseph Ltd

PRINTING HISTORY
Michael Joseph edition published 1986
Bantam edition published 1992

Set in 11/13pt Times by Kestrel Data, Exeter

Bantam Books are published by Transworld Publishers Ltd.,
61–63 Uxbridge Road, Ealing, London W5 5SA, in Australia by
Transworld Publishers (Australia) Pty. Ltd., 15–23 Helles
Avenue, Moorebank, NSW 2170, and in New Zealand by
Transworld Publishers (NZ) Ltd., 3 William Pickering Drive,
Albany, Auckland.

Made and printed in Great Britain by
Cox & Wyman Ltd., Reading, Beds.

# Time – Not the Present

# 1

'You have to be very rich to enjoy the simple things of life,' sighed Lady Pemberton.

She pulled the last of the early spring carrots out of the flinty Wiltshire soil and popped them into her trug. They were a pretty sight, even though orange was not really her colour.

She started to walk up towards the house, stopping every now and then to look at a plant or a shrub that needed tidying. She did like a 'tidy' garden, quite unlike the garden that she had inherited, where plants were allowed to tumble and climbing roses spread through trees and along walls with a carelessness that was quite horrifying to someone such as herself, brought up surrounded by the strict garden architecture of Surrey's commuter belt.

When she had first arrived at the Hall, a very new Marchioness, she had wrought many changes in the grounds, all of them she was quite sure for the better, but it seemed that the Seventh Marquis, her husband, after a short honeymoon period during which he had allowed her free rein, was now determined to be at odds with her about everything, most of all the garden. He must have carelessness. He must have things trailing. He must have old-fashioned scents. He must have borders that were quite definitely a nightmare of untidiness to her. For as fast as she ordered the gardener and his boy to snip and hack, so equally Pember, with some sixth sense that was so dreadfully irritating, would appear from nowhere (sometimes even when he was meant to be safely on the train to London) and countermand her orders, until in the end it seemed that the garden at the Hall must always be an unfortunate misalliance between the niceties of Surrey and the artlessness of Wiltshire.

Jennifer of course was only too aware of it, but never more than when her mother came to see her on a visit. She stopped and put her trug down, and pushed her arms into a cashmere cardigan. Just remembering her mother on a visit brought about little feelings of chill. It wasn't that the former Mrs Parker-Jones was particularly vicious in her comments, it was the fact that she did not comment at all. She made little noises instead, noises that you had to interpret for yourself. Little murmurs that boded ill for a clematis here, a daphne there. Jennifer had to give it to her mother, the present Mrs Andrew Gillott, that she had made the practice of saying nothing, and therefore meaning more, into a minor art.

Up at the house Jennifer handed the butler her trug. It was a familiar little ceremony, and one which they re-enacted almost daily throughout the summer. Jennifer might not garden, but she did like to pick the fruits of other people's labours.

Bloss took the trug as he always did, as if he had not realised that vegetables came from the garden; as if until that moment he had always thought they grew in little frozen bags you emptied into water.

'Thank you, m'lady,' said Bloss, not meaning it in the least.

Jennifer walked slowly up the polished wooden stairs to her bedroom. She thought she would brush her hair before lunch and re-read the letter she had received that morning from her friend the former Lady Georgiana Longborough, now the Third Baroness Stranragh.

It was a letter that gave Jennifer great satisfaction for many reasons. It was long, which must mean Georgiana was lonely. It was full of descriptions of the Scottish countryside, which must mean she was bored; and it made frequent reference to her husband, which must mean that they were not getting on.

Georgiana had been very kind to Jennifer at school (Grantley Abbey) and had even gone on to be kind to her afterwards, before Jennifer's marriage to John Pemberton, the Seventh Marquis of that name. She had been kind to her in the way that a beautiful girl can always afford to be kind to a plain one, which is to say that she had not minded in the least going to parties with her; and when Jennifer married 'well', Georgiana had been 'pleased', even though Pemberton and Georgiana had been a little more than just good friends in the recent past. Now, it seemed to Jennifer, it would be quite safe to be kind back to Georgiana, for living in Scotland was not enviable, what with the flies and people only going to stay with you if they could kill things.

'The longest day of the week' wrote Georgiana, 'is usually Sunday. Here it is like Sunday every day !!!!! James is always busy killing things !!!!!!!'

Jennifer stared at the plethora of exclamation marks.

9

There were five after 'day' and seven after 'things'. Even she knew that this was a sign of hysteria.

'I have a pony and trap, and an Irish wolfhound for company. The village think the Castle are mad.'

Jennifer felt a little lift at the idea that Georgiana might be going mad. It would be terribly appropriate, like the naked Lady Caroline Lamb stepping out of that dish at that dinner party.

Jennifer arose from the cushioned window seat and walked purposefully towards her early-eighteenth-century escritoire. She must reply to Georgiana's missive at once, not by sending her a letter crammed with news, but by asking her to stay. The news could wait for her ladyship to discover for herself. She carefully unscrewed the top of her gold Lady Sheaffer pen, and taking a sheet of paper that had a drawing of the Hall elegantly engraved upon the top, she wrote to Georgiana and invited her to stay. Warm but to the point, her letter was without exclamation marks. She finished the letter, and then, licking the envelope briefly, she put it aside for Bloss to take to the village on his horrid little Honda.

And now for lunch, a meal for which she had no affection whatsoever, but upon which Pember insisted. Sometimes, oh joy, on the days that he went to London, she was able to skip the beastly meal, or climb the nursery stairs and bake some fish fingers on the Baby Belling with Nanny, but today, alas, was not one of those days; today would be Pember and a thin consommé, and proper fish, and Pember talking about deadly dull things that had no interest for her, such as which stallion he had decided to send his favourite mare to, or in which catalogue he had found some boring rare shrub. For not

10

only was Pember a gardening bore, being able to reel off the names of all the plants, Latin *intacta*, but he was a 'breeding bore'. Quite frankly, sometimes she honestly thought she would rather have had a husband who was a golfing bore, for she couldn't imagine that hearing about bogeys or birdies, or holes in one, would be as stultifying as hearing about whom a horse or a mare was out of; and it wasn't as if they ever managed to prove anything when they did actually produce some sort of a winner. No, it seemed to prove nothing at all, except a whole set of new questions as to where they should put this one in foal, or whatever. She had come to dread the words 'out of' in the same way some other wretched wife might come to dread 'bulls and bears' or 'profit and loss', the one difference being that if you were married to a horse bore he did at least change his conversation slightly in the evening, once he had seen the racing results.

Lunch at the Hall was never therefore a very joyous affair. Pember there to eat, Jennifer to avoid eating. Pember wanting to drone, Jennifer wanting to avoid listening. Today, perhaps because her early carrots were looking really rather succulent on their Wedgwood plate, Jennifer decided to direct the conversation herself, and to stick to it firmly, no matter what Pember's feelings might be.

'I think Bloss has itchy feet,' said Jennifer, once he had withdrawn with the heated trolley. And then, having said that, she stared at her fork, which still had little blobs of pink silver polish in between the prongs.

She actually didn't think that Bloss did have itchy feet, but she wanted to distract Pember from her main intention, and mentioning Bloss and even the remote possibility that he would not always be part of Pember's life was enough to soften him up to the point of hysteria. In fact Bloss had not been all that he should be lately (witness the lamentable state of her fork), but she thought it might be more to do with his spending too much time down at the Queen's Arms rather than anything else, though she was not going to tell Pember this.

'Of course he could earn six times as much as you pay him in America,' Jennifer added.

'America. Bloss wouldn't like America,' said Pemberton through rather too large a mouthful. 'Besides, he's said nothing to me about wanting more than he's getting. Nothing at all.'

'I think he's bored,' Jennifer persisted.

'Bored? Here? Nonsense. He's got no reason to be bored here,' said Pemberton, shocked.

'Oh yes he has.'

'What do you mean "oh yes he has"?'

'What I said – "oh yes he has".'

'Yes, but what does it mean? Explain yourself.'

'Too little variety,' said Jennifer with relish, and then having crossed her t's and dotted her i's to her own satisfaction, she helped herself to some very dull water biscuits that were Pember's favourites.

'He can't be bored here, he's got everything that he could possibly want.'

'In America he could have a swimming pool of his own.'

'He doesn't swim.'

'That's not the point,' said Jennifer.

'You're making him out to be the kind of person that I know he's not. Bloss is not the kind of chap that sits about longing for a pool when he can't swim.'

Jennifer now said nothing, but merely smiled. In Pemberton's opinion, Jennifer's silent smiles should be grounds for divorce. He could never understand people who admired that picture *La Giaconda*, not once you'd lived with your own version. Women smiling mysteriously might do something for other men, but they did nothing for him, except make his blood pressure go up to unacceptable levels.

For the next few minutes, while Jennifer crackled her way through the water biscuits, Pemberton brooded. Of course Jennifer might be right. She often was. Not that it made her any the less irritating, but on occasions when she had been right there had been terrible consequences. Perhaps Bloss would like a motor car instead of his Honda? He couldn't offer him a swimming pool, because – well, it would be an embarrassment to both of them making Pemberton look as if he were willing to go to any lengths to keep his butler, and Bloss would look a fool, because he couldn't swim. Such, however, could not be said for a good motor car. No, that would probably do the trick. He'd be able to get around better, combat this boredom, or whatever was troubling him.

Jennifer paused by the door.

'Oh, Pember?'

'Yes, my sweet?'

'By the way, I don't think I told you but I've asked Georgiana to stay in a couple of weeks' time, so if you want to go off, you know, somewhere, for something, you know fishing, or whatever, it might be a good idea.'

13

'Yes, yes, of course.'

Pemberton nodded distractedly. Jennifer smiled again, and then left the dining room humming a brief snatch from the Grantley Abbey school song. 'Up, up, to higher things, aim girls aim.' She had aimed, fired, and hit her target. Most satisfactory.

Georgiana received the Seventh Marchioness of Pemberton's letter four days after Bloss had posted it in the wall by the Queen's Arms. She noticed that it had taken four days to arrive in spite of its having been sent by first class mail. She knew that it was as much part of her present existence to notice such things as it had been part of her past existence not to notice such things. Just as she now noticed that her husband was squeaking his fork upon his breakfast plate, and delaying the moment when he would ask whom the letter was from.

'To have and to hold from this day forward, including all my letters.'

If she had known just how public marriage was going to be, she could never have said 'I will' in her family church at Longborough to James Charles Arthur Stranragh, the Third Baron to hold that title.

She pushed the letter slowly back into its coroneted envelope. She would very much like to leave Scotland, even for a week, even to stay with Jennifer, but she knew that she must not let Stranragh know this. It would be enough for him to discover that she wanted to go somewhere for pleasure, for him to try and stop her. For him it would have to be a 'need', not a pleasure.

'The second button on your blouse is undone.'

'Thank you.'

14

Georgiana did up the button. He had broken the silence, so it would definitely not be long before he asked her for her letter, but first a pause as he looked her over. Mentally she called it 'breakfast assembly'. Every night she spent a great deal of time carefully choosing her clothes for 'breakfast assembly'.

Down to the table last every day, she would wait for him to comment, not pleasurably, but just to comment on what she was wearing. She had always been taught to take 'correction well', so she took Stranragh's little corrections very well. This morning a button, one of twenty-four little silk buttons that did up her blouse, had come undone; yesterday it had been a crease in her skirt, and the day before he had not liked her shoes.

She did up her button, and then waited in the deafening silence that followed for him to demand her letter.

'May I see your letter?'

He read it, then folded it and put it back into the envelope. Not as it had been, but half sticking out. She wondered if this meant that he had not liked what he had read?

'So Jennifer Pemberton wants you to go and stay with her?'

'Yes.'

'Do you want to go?'

'Not particularly.'

Georgiana's hands pressed down against her hip bones, which since her marriage had begun to stick out more and more visibly.

'I think you should go.'

'But it's such a long way.'

15

'It would be good for you.'

It would be good for her like black molasses, and kneeling on peas, and going to bed without supper.

'No, I don't think I will, if you don't mind, James, thank you.'

'I shall be going to London. It will involve no extra expense. I think you should go. You look pale.'

'I've always been pale.'

'You look more pale than you have been before.'

'I am perfectly well.'

'I know you are perfectly well, but the winter here is long, and in the South—'

Georgiana's imagination followed his use of the word 'south'. South as in South West One. South as in the warm, the blushful hippocrene. South as in the South of France. South as in where she had been happy.

'I think you should go. You need a change.'

'I don't feel as if I need a change.'

'Perhaps not, but you look as if you need a change.'

Stranragh arose from the table. He always arose, leaving his napkin in a little heap and pushing his chair back to the precise spot from which he had removed it. Then he left the room as quietly as he had entered it. He did everything quietly, as if he had been trained never to disturb anything by movement. Georgiana had learnt never not to expect to see him, nor to take it for granted that he had gone. Just as she had learnt not to think in front of him, for she feared that he had ways of knowing what she thought, and then other ways of punishing her for those thoughts.

She hated Scotland. She hated Scotland as much as it was possible to hate anything other than poverty –

which she had never known but which she had feared as much as she now feared Stranragh. She did not fear him in her thoughts, because instinctively she knew that to fear him in her thoughts would mean discovery; she actually feared him physically. A tense draining sort of fear that made her expect him any moment at any time, that didn't quite trust him to go away completely, not even now, so that when she opened the dining room door she half-expected him to be behind it, and when she went down the long dark castle corridors towards the kitchens she half-expected him to be there too, and behind the old green baize door and beyond the cellars where she kept her Irish wolfhound.

'Such a strange dog to have in Scotland,' her mother-in-law remarked.

The Dowager Lady Stranragh, the second wife of the second baron, was a raven-haired woman who wore her now greying hair in heavy plaits around her head. 'Lady Georgiana', as she always referred to Georgiana, supposedly humorously, was not the sort of girl of whom the Dowager could approve. A girl with her roots in the South, a London girl who only weekended in the country, a girl who wore lipstick to chapel, and stockings with little bows on the heels.

'No babies yet, Lady Georgiana?' she would ask on her monthly visit. And then she would make a little sucking noise, and waggle her head sideways in a way that Georgiana thought made her look distinctly hennish.

Step-mama was the only person to whom Stranragh deferred. He was always up a little earlier before her visit. Always a little longer checking the menu with Mrs Peebles. And, of course, the wine; for although the

Dowager did not approve of the new Lady Stranragh, and although her allegiance to the kirk was total, she did enjoy a glass of wine.

She never came unaccompanied on her visits, but would bring her sewing in a bag and position herself in a winged chair beside the fire, and having draped some silks over the arm, would sew and talk in the same way that she must have sewn and talked when Stranragh's father was alive. She positioned herself so that the rest of the room became cold, so that no one else could see the fire, and so that Georgiana became a visitor in her own house and she the châtelaine; and James accepted that she did this, as meekly as if he was still only a boy in his father's house.

Georgiana went into the stable yard to collect her dog. A cold breeze was blowing even though it was well past spring. She shivered.

'Summer in Scotland arrives around the twentieth of June, and is over by the fifteenth of August,' her step-mother-in-law liked to intone. And then she would look at 'Lady Georgiana' with brown-eyed malice, knowing that, although Georgiana would never admit it, she was thin-skinned and felt the cold dreadfully.

Before her marriage to James, Georgiana had imagined her life in Scotland as promising to be a mixture of Lorna Doone and life at Balmoral when Prince Albert was still alive. And indeed, with this in mind, she had had her portrait painted (white dress with tartan sash) and hung in the Blue Drawing Room, and she had learnt to drive a pony and trap; and all this during her honeymoon, which she spent in the confident belief that her days in Scotland were numbered, and that as soon as her husband took it upon himself, he would declare the thing officially over and pull up stumps, and she could return with some relief to his house in London, her house in the country, or his house in Italy. None of these happy ideas about the future came to pass, for no sooner had the metaphysical portcullis at the Castle closed behind her than Georgiana discovered that the Third Baron Stranragh had no more intention of returning to London than she had had of remaining in Scotland. Her husband being the sort of person that he was, she came to understand that it would be made very difficult for her to do as she wished.

No-one who has not been unhappily married can prepare themselves for the intensities of misunderstanding that can follow the happy exit of the bride through the church doors on the arm of her husband. Georgiana was certainly no exception. She was as unprepared for marriage as any person must be who has only imagined the clothes that she will wear in her future life, but not the emotions that will accompany the clothes. Fantasies of tartan sashes and white dresses are of little use when there is only your dog for company, and your husband killing rabbits in the grounds.

Georgiana started to walk towards the distant hills. The intensity of her longing to escape from Stranragh and his castle was so overpowering that she found that she had walked a great deal further than she had intended before she saw on her watch that it was lunchtime, and Stranragh would be waiting for her.

'So you'll be going to stay with the Pembertons, then.' Stranragh raised the subject once again at lunch, as Georgiana knew that he would.

She took a little sip of barley water, and then said, 'Oh, I don't think so.'

'I do. Yes, I really think so.'

Stranragh sighed. Georgiana tried not to smile. She knew that sigh. It meant that he thought he was pushing her to do something that she did not want. And then he would press his thin lips together, and discourage further discussion.

James was aware that he was frightening. He was as aware of it as someone of great beauty would be aware of that. No-one, she often thought, who had never lived with someone frightening could imagine what that quality was. Something intangible, insistent, immutable, inarguable, manic, and ultimately bad. Frightening people were able to make life unbearable for everyone unless they had their way, and in James's case his 'way' was always something that he thought Georgiana would not like. She pressed her hands into her hip bones again.

'I don't really want to go, I don't really like Jennifer Pemberton very much,' she said, much as she would have said the same thing to Nanny.

'No, I really think you must go.'

For the second time that day Stranragh rose from the table. Georgiana watched him. Her excitement was so intense she felt she might be sick. If he got to the door without changing his mind she knew she would have fooled him. He reached the door, opened it, and closed it quietly behind him. It seemed that for the first time for two years it was she who had got her way. She got up from the table and, throwing her napkin down, she too left the dining room.

*     *     *

Once Pemberton had been sent to fish with some boring old friend of his in Devon, Jennifer started to relax and enjoy herself. Men were a great big nuisance if you had a girlfriend to stay. They got all jealous and silly, and would do immensely irritating things to make the visit a flop, things that they normally always accused girls of; like correcting your stories, or insisting on making everyone go to bed early. So having waved Pemberton off for his week in thigh-high wellies, she turned her attention to Georgiana's projected visit. Happily the menus were not a consideration, not when girlfriends were staying, for they never minded what they ate, just so long as it wasn't very much; but there were the flowers, and the linen, and also what might be called 'conversational' strategy, for Jennifer was determined to find out everything that she could about Georgiana. An exciting challenge, for Georgiana was not someone who 'gave away a lot'.

The day of the visit dawned bright and clear, just like in a play. It couldn't have been better really, thought Jennifer. For once the Hall would be seen to its best advantage; usually they had only to allow the grounds to be used for a fête, and lo and behold the heavens would open. Now, with the sun risen and giving out a nice comfortable memsahib kind of heat, she was able to pose on the lawn with her tapestry frame and her straw hat, without any fear of rain, or any other kind of 'real' weather. Even her wools stayed quite nice and still on the arm of her white, wooden, Chinese Chippendale bench.

As soon as Bloss showed Georgiana into the garden Jennifer knew that it would not be difficult for her to discover the exact state of Georgiana's marriage. It was all too evident in Georgiana's emaciated frame.

'My goodness, you're whippet thin,' said Jennifer, quite giving up any pretence at not 'noticing'.

Georgiana smiled slightly.

'It suits you,' said Jennifer graciously.

'It hurts to sit down,' said Georgiana. 'My bones stick into the chairs.'

'Never mind, I'll get a lovely comfy Peter Rabbit cushion from my little tea hut, and then they won't,' said Jennifer, her maternal instinct instantly aroused by such a predicament.

She hurried off to what she called her 'little tea hut', and as she hurried she allowed herself a little private gasp. She had rarely seen marriage take such a toll on anyone as it had on Georgiana. Of course, strictly speaking, she was still beautiful, but not the kind of beauty that men admire. More the kind of beauty that girls admire, where all your clothes are falling off you and your eyes have that haunted look reminiscent of charity posters.

She hurried back with her favourite Peter Rabbit cushion, and patted it into place. Even so Georgiana sat down with great care, as if she expected pain.

'Bloss is going to bring us out a lovely Pimms,' said Jennifer in the voice that she normally only used to the children when she wanted them to eat up, or hurry up.

There was a small silence as Georgiana looked round the garden as if she could hardly believe she was there. Jennifer's eyes followed her gaze, and she found her own had tears in them. There was something so pathetic about the way Georgiana was gazing about her, as if she had been in prison, or in hospital for a long time, and had never hoped to see a Wiltshire garden again.

'Oh look, here's Bloss, with the Pimms,' said Jennifer which was silly, but she couldn't think of anything else to say.

She had, quite frankly, never been so relieved to see anyone. She didn't normally feel at a loss nowadays, not at home anyway, nor did she normally feel like a drink at midday, but Georgiana's appearance had quite thrown her.

'Oh Blossy, could you bring out some snacky things to go with the Pimms?'

Bloss looked across at Jennifer.

'*Bloss*,' he said heavily, 'will, m'lady.'

Jennifer nodded. 'Lady Georgiana needs feeding up,' she said, to excuse her verbal confusions. And then she gave Bloss one of her 'just between me and you' looks, because she never normally called him 'Blossy', but what with one thing and another the lovely calm feeling that she had had before Georgiana's arrival had quite *disparu*.

'I never thought I'd get out,' said Georgiana.

'What of? The car?'

'No, not the car,' said Georgiana in a low voice. 'Scotland.'

'Doesn't James *ever* want to leave?' asked Jennifer.

Georgiana looked at her. She could never explain to Jennifer what being married to 'James' was like. Even the way Jennifer said 'James', so crisply, so dismissively, even that made Georgiana realise that Jennifer would never have allowed James to be as he had been to Georgiana. Jennifer had not Georgiana's burden of

23

beauty. She had never been a beauty. (Although now, after a duet of children, she did seem to have a bloom and a confidence that were very charming.) And sitting on her lawn with her tapestry wools and her frame, her plump arms composed about her person and her straw hat protecting her fair skin, she had the composure sometimes glimpsed in old portraits. Chip straw hats, cherries, muslin, black ribbon, lace, and *fichus*, all these came to mind when the onlooker gazed upon Jennifer that morning.

Because Georgiana had not answered her question Jennifer sipped her Pimms through a bendy straw, and then started the conversation again.

'You must make James leave Scotland,' she said. 'You must be firm. Men are much stuffier than women, and they need to be pushed to do things. It took me some time to find this out myself, but if left to himself, the average man will just spend his time racing, fishing, shooting and collecting art, and give no thought whatsoever to the great responsibilities that marriage brings. Do you know, I have to beg Pember to read to the boys? No, I mean it, "beg", as on "bended knees". I mean he was so thrilled to have babies, but once they arrived I think he expected them to grow under glass like his wretched tomatoes. No, firmness is needed. After all no sane person I know ever spends more than a month a year in Scotland. It's not as if James hasn't got other houses, is it? Or as if you couldn't go to Longborough, even if he didn't want to, I mean at least you could go, couldn't you?'

Jennifer was aware that she was talking far too much, but she didn't care. It gave her time to think. She poured another drink out for Georgiana who had finished hers, and topped up her own. She must get Georgiana to talk, and Pimms might be the way.

Now she left a silence. Georgiana turned to look at the garden.

'It's hardly summer yet in Scotland,' she said, half to herself.

'How do you stand the flies?' asked Jennifer, knowing that this would be emotive.

'I stay indoors.'

'No wonder you look so pale,' said Jennifer. 'I don't know, what with both the flies and the cold keeping you indoors, no wonder you look as if you need a holiday.'

'Do you mind if we walk round the garden? My bones are hurting.'

Jennifer took Georgiana's arm, and they started to walk.

'You're going to need a rubber ring to sit on, like the ones they give you on the maternity ward,' she said.

For the first time since her arrival Georgiana laughed, and Jennifer squeezed her arm slightly. They were not yet at an age when all feminine rivalry could be put behind them, but even so they were old enough to appreciate how much they had been through together, and Jennifer was determined that whatever it was that Georgiana had been through with James, it was going to have to stop. Her imagination wandered a little as they discussed flowers. He couldn't beat her surely, because the marks would show somewhere. He might be a sadist though, like the kind that held orgies in Hell Fire Caves and told you all about it later. Or he might be just very unkind, which although dull, is far from being so to live with. In fact, she once knew a girl whose hair fell out as a result of her husband's unkind remarks.

'I expect you're wondering why I look so dreadful?' said Georgiana.

Jennifer would have liked to deny it, but that would have been silly, since it was all too evident that Georgiana was looking dreadful.

Georgiana stopped walking. She couldn't look at Jennifer. Somehow her plump, anxious, homely expression took her so sharply back to the dear days of Grantley Abbey that it brought a lump to her throat.

She started to laugh.

Jennifer thought immediately, 'a mild form of hysteria'.

'What's the matter?' she asked.

'Nothing.'

But Georgiana went on laughing.

'It's just that you look exactly as you used to at the Abbey, when you let a goal through.'

Now Jennifer had to laugh.

'Oh dear,' she said. 'And the size I was you would have thought nothing could have got past me, wouldn't you?'

They both laughed, and then stopped.

Jennifer wanted to say 'what *does* he do to you?', but she just couldn't bring herself to, in case that would be enough to stop Georgiana saying any more.

'I don't know how I've survived the last months.'

Georgiana walked on through the wild garden. Jennifer, having plucked a nasty looking weed out of one of the borders, quickly followed her. She knew from that remark that it would not be long before the secret of Georgiana's marriage would be out. What a relief it would be for her to confide in Jennifer, Jennifer thought. And how riveting it would be to listen. For the moment, however, it would not be right to look too interested.

'You see,' Georgiana said, still walking ahead, 'I did think I loved James before I married him.'

'We all do,' said Jennifer warmly.

'And he certainly loved me.'

'I know. I remember you wrote to me all about those lovely clothes he bought you, and the jewels from Florence.'

'He seemed very passionate.'

Jennifer now stooped to pluck another weed from another flower bed. Her least favourite, full of untidy choices and plants that defied neatening.

'But from our wedding night on I realised that I was quite mistaken. I mean, you can imagine, if your wedding night is a flop—'

Georgiana did not finish her sentence, but for the first time looked Jennifer full in the face. Once more Jennifer's maternal instinct came to the fore. Her feelings for Georgiana had always been tempered by Georgiana's beauty. She had always suspected that Georgiana had used Jennifer's homely looks to set off her own, in the way that a plinth does a vase of flowers, but now she felt as close to her as women do in pregnancy.

'My wedding night was a flop too,' Jennifer said. 'Pember all drunk and silly, and never noticing my White House negligée. I shouldn't worry about that.'

'I shouldn't have either. Except that every night since then has been a "wedding night",' Georgiana added.

'Surely not?'

'Oh yes.'

There was a small silence as they walked on up the lawn. Jennifer thought quickly. Did this mean that Georgiana was neglected, or merely dissatisfied? Without realizing it, she wrinkled her nose slightly. She did not like 'frank discussions' unless they were about childbirth, or how to avoid operations by taking herbal remedies, just general topics like that. Discussions about what people did to each other and when were not to her taste.

'He simply doesn't want to know.'

Put tactfully like that, Jennifer felt quite able to continue the conversation.

'My goodness.'

'That would be bad enough, but there is worse. You see he torments me about it. He blames me. He says I'm not attractive to him, that I'm insensitive, that I need – well, that it's my fault.'

'Typical male,' Jennifer snorted, and then moved quickly towards the table with the Pimms because all this news was making her thirsty.

She poured them both two large drinks and then sat down, patting the Peter Rabbit cushion for Georgiana.

'Of course it's all nonsense,' she said, suddenly sounding, even to herself, just like Pember. 'Sheer nonsense. He can't possibly put the blame on you because he's not able to be a man, and from the sound of it he's not even a gentleman either.'

Georgiana laughed, and then wiped a tear from her eye.

'You don't know what being here, with you, *not* being

in Scotland, you don't know what it means to me. I never thought I'd ever get out.'

'And from the look of you I don't think you should ever go back,' said Jennifer. 'Not ever.'

'I don't want to, not ever.'

'Then you shan't,' said Jennifer decisively. 'You shall stay here with Pember and me.'

Then she remembered that Georgiana had had a tiny affair-thing with Pember, and so she added just in time, 'Well, anyway, until we get things sorted out.'

# 2

Flint House was necessarily a focus of attention for the village, for its occupants were two confirmed bachelors, one of whom had married the pregnant widow of Sir Gerard Tisbury. Perhaps if the bachelors had not been so confirmed in their status before the unexpected marriage, the village, and in particular the regulars at the Queen's Arms, would not have been so interested; but since both Fulton and Elliott had been employed as interior decorators by both the late, largely unlamented Sir Gerard, and the village's very own Marchioness of Pemberton, it was obvious to all that if reassurance was needed on any point, it was definitely not needed for this.

'If any of them's got our Lady Tizzy in the family way, then my sprouts is onions,' was how one of her more rural Wiltshire neighbours put it.

Irene in the village shop said, and she said it daily, shouting over the noise of her hand-operated till, that funnier things had happened, but usually only at sea.

Still, although the humour was rife and ribald, there was a certain loyalty to Lady Tizzy, for ever since she had first entered their lives clothed from head to toe in black leather, Lady Tizzy had provided as much interest as, and sometimes perhaps slightly more than, the television. Nor were they now able to change her name, for 'Lady Tizzy' would always be 'Lady Tizzy' to them, even though she was now, legally, Mrs Montrose-Benedict-Cavanagh.

The village was not alone in their inability to think of her as anything but 'Lady Tizzy'; her present husband, Fulton, was also unable to think of her in any other way, and had even booked her into the Countryside Clinic under her former married name.

'Of course the baby will be christened Montrose-Benedict-Cavanagh, or rather, something, something Montrose-Benedict-Cavanagh, but that's different,' said Elliott.

'Something, something, something Montrose-Benedict-Cavanagh,' said Fulton, correcting him.

They had both spent the entire winter arguing over names. Elliott had maintained, with some justification, that there wouldn't be room for *three* names and *three* surnames. Fulton, who had added at least two of his own surnames, did not agree. Happily they were united on one more important point, they both wanted a girl. In fact, they both wanted a girl so much they had been quite unable to find any boys' names suitable, although Fulton favoured Peregrine, and Elliott had to admit that Perry Montrose-Benedict-Cavanagh did have a certain cachet to it.

Neither of them liked to think of Patti suffering at all while delivering 'their baby', and so the best was only just good enough for her. First of all a nice airy ground-floor room with bathroom en suite in the Clinic, and then slightly private preparation classes from the woman in the village who ran the playgroup. Elliott, who took the medical side of the whole future event a great deal more seriously than Fulton, accompanied Patti to her classes. They did deep breathing on the old school-room floor, together with three very large ladies from the neighbouring village, and Elliott played softly to them during 'rest time' on an old upright piano, which hurt his fingers.

'You've not seen what lack of co-ordination means,' he told Fulton, 'until you've seen Mrs R and Mrs D blithely lifting up their legs in answer to a request to stretch out their arms.'

Sometimes it seemed to Fulton that it was Elliott not Patti who was about to give birth, so full was he of the expected arrival. Even his skin seemed to have taken on an added bloom.

'Are you going to have contractions too, when the time comes?' he asked him.

Elliott picked up a pair of nail scissors and snipped off a few leaves from a butterfly plant.

'It's possible,' he threatened.

'I'm not sure I can cope,' Fulton sighed.

They had all the rooms ready for the baby, for the monthly nurse, and for the nanny, who had been highly recommended by someone with a title that no-one had ever heard of, but who sounded stuffy enough to be the kind of person who would not tolerate anything untoward or excessive in nannies. The walls of the day nursery had been ragrolled in a tasteful pale yellow, and then touches of grey and yellow picked out in the furniture, together with a sort of cerise colour echoed in the sashes and swags on the curtains. The cot had been sewn by Elliott himself, copying one he had seen in France (supposedly used for the offspring of one of the Ducs de Berry, although which Duc Elliott could never quite remember).

'Too good for a baby, really,' said Patti when she saw it.

And Fulton privately agreed, but he would not hurt Elliott's feelings by saying so. He himself had contributed to the general expectancy by painting a mural of animals in the nursery bathroom complete with chubby-bottomed flower fairies. In the corner he put a little pair of dancing shoes. When Patti saw it she cried a little, but not so much as to make her nose red which Fulton would not like. Now that she was too fat to touch her toes, or even as Elliott said, anyone else's, she loved to remember her days as a Bluebell girl.

'But supposing he's a boy?'

'What matter,' said Fulton, 'he could still be a Nijinsky or a Balanchine.'

'Oh I don't think we'd want him to be anything foreign,' said Patti.

Fulton patted the top of her head fondly. There was something so restful about Patti's stupidity. It didn't make her aggressive as it did other people. And although she was beautiful her beauty never seemed to make her want to 'score', or make other people feel less because of it. Over the previous months Fulton had come to realise that she was, in fact, that most maligned of individuals, a nice person.

Of course the village was agog with the excitement of the birth, for with the sole exception of the Pembertons up at the Hall, new babies were an infrequent occurrence among a population whose average age was well over the speed limit allowed in built-up areas. Unlike the occupants of Flint House, however, the interest of the village was not centred on the sex of Lady Tizzy's baby, but upon who the possible father might have been, for 'been he is, and gone he is, of that you can be sure', was how they put it at the Queen's Arms.

Obviously Patti could have put the village out of suspense, but since Fulton had been courteous enough to marry her and the baby now had a 'name', as she put it, she really didn't see that the question of the child's actual paternity had any remaining importance, least of all to it, or to her.

'And if I *hadn't* married you,' Fulton asked her every now and then, 'what would you have done?'

'I would have pretended it was Knightey's,' she would answer, somewhat ingenuously, for the late Sir Gerard had departed this life far too soon to be anything but a far too 'late' father of her baby.

'I've got a feeling no-one would have believed you,' said Fulton.

'Why ever not? The gynaecologist says that virgin births are two a penny.'

'I think it might have been a tiny bit difficult for you to have put in such a claim.'

'Well, you know what I mean.'

'I might do, but thousands wouldn't. Anyway there still has to be a father even with a "virgin birth", as you call it.'

At this point the conversation would become too complicated for Patti, and she would turn a little restlessly to the television and a programme of her choice, usually something for the 'younger viewer'.

This particular day Fulton found her watching *Pogley*

*and the Peg Tops* and singing along, quite tunefully and
sweetly, with Pogley. Once Pogley had finished, he leant
forward and switched the programme off.

'Time for your rest.'

'Already?'

'Any little pains or anything?'

'Not a thing.'

'Never mind, won't be long.'

He kissed the top of her head.

'Don't forget to take off your pregnancy tights,' he
called after her, 'and your shoes,' he added, and then
gave a small sigh. After all anything was possible with
Patti, no not possible, probable.

Patti climbed the stairs to her bedroom with her usual
feeling of gratitude. Her new husband, unlike her old
one, was ideal. Not that she hadn't loved her old one,
but he had had, if she was to be frank, some very
demanding habits, none of which, upon reflection, she
actually missed. Nowadays she could sleep undisturbed
in her own bedroom with her own bathroom (all beautifully redecorated in Colefax and Fowler chintz) and
know that when she awoke she could look forward to a
day which would contain nothing of greater import than
watching telly and practising her breathing exercises
with Elliott. There was no use denying that to a person
of her outlook it was the ideal existence.

'You're so deeply shallow,' Elliott would sigh after
writing down her order for Adult Romance from Stanton.

'Someone's got to be,' said Patti, 'otherwise there'd
be even more lack of jobs, wouldn't there?'

'With which logic,' as Fulton said, 'one cannot
somehow find an argument.'

Naturally the nursery suite had not been the only focus of attention at Flint House. The house itself had been badly in need of re-modelling, and re-furnishing, for although Fulton had been in charge of redecorating it for Patti's late husband Sir Gerard, the taste that he had exercised to please an ageing baronet and his young wife was not the taste that either he or Elliott could find compatible with their own. To be truthful, they had had to start all over again. The swan-shaped taps with gold-plated fitments were replaced, to Patti's bewilderment, by old brass taps that ran rusty water. The corner bath by one with claw feet. All the telephones were replaced, leaving only Patti's (her favourite Boudoir Fone shaped in the image of a woman's hand with mock emeralds in the handpiece) and that was just the start.

'I hardly know my way around any more,' she complained to Irene in the shop.

'Well, you wouldn't, would you?' said Irene. 'I know I can never remember where I've put anything when I've fallen for a baby.'

'Everything's a different shape, even,' said Patti, choosing some tinned apricots from one of the shelves.

'I shouldn't let it worry you, dear, so long as you're not in pain. That's all that matters.'

'Busy, busy, busy is what we've been,' said Elliott proudly when he showed their old friend the Countess round.

'So I see,' said the Countess, who had thought it was high time that she came down from London to see what was what. 'Those legs are all wrong,' she added, pointing to a piece that was being re-made in the stable workshop.

'Not for Sheraton, surely?'

'Do you know I once worked out that if Sheraton had made every piece attributed to him he'd have died at the age of seven hundred and eight?'

'Really?' said Elliott, feigning disinterest, but quickly remembering the remark to re-use himself.

'What do you think of our new line in nineteenth-century coffee tables for California? We make the legs from old newel posts.'

'Disgusting,' said the Countess.

'Yes, they are rather, aren't they?'

'You should have horses in your stables, not little men faking furniture.'

'Yes, I suppose, but then we have to think of the baby, and its future. Can't quite afford to go bankrupt now.'

The Countess did not reply, being still of the opinion that money was not something a person should discuss. She was not in her best mood, but stayed for tea, during which time both Fulton and Elliott prayed silently that Patti and her pregnancy would remain upstairs.

'She doesn't approve, does she?'

Fulton waved at her departing car, and then shut the front door carefully and quietly behind them because they wanted Patti to get as much sleep as possible.

'No, she doesn't approve,' agreed Elliott, 'but worse than that – she doesn't *like*.'

'Having too good a time?'

'Precisely.'

'She can see the bluebird of happiness sitting on our roof, and that is not good.'

'No, it's not, is it?'

'Angels and ministers of God defend us.'

37

'Quite. I just wish that I didn't think He might have other things on His mind.'

They cleared the Wedgwood cups that had been used for tea, and then Elliott laid a new tray for Patti's 'late tea': her special china cup with harvest mice on it filled with instant coffee made with milk, and two bourbon biscuits that it was her habit to dunk in the Nescafé.

'Scratch, scratch, it's Ely-ot,' said Elliott.

Inside her bedroom Patti hastily hid the now nearly finished tin of apricots.

'Come in, Ely-ot,' she called after a moment.

Elliott put the tray down on the mahogany stool at the foot of the bed and went, with light tread, to pull the curtains.

'And how's m'lady now?' he asked.

'Bit blooming uncomfortable,' said Patti.

Elliott sighed slightly. Patti's lack of style was something of an anxiety to both Fulton and himself. Try as they could to give her polish, she was somehow resistant to veneer.

'Guess what?'

'Don't know?'

'A parcel for you.'

Elliott put it down in front of her.

'Oh sure. Thanks.'

Patti looked at it incuriously, and then put it on one of the dress tables beside her.

'Can't I know?'

'Oh, it's nothing. Just something I sent for.'

Elliott held out her special cup, and smiled. He knew she ate tinned apricots in bed, and before long, whether she liked it or not, he would discover what was in the parcel, but until then he was quite content to be patient. He smiled at her.

'Come on, drink up before it gets a skin.'

Elliott left Patti obediently dunking her biscuits in her cup and went downstairs, quite loudly. Once at the bottom of the stairs, he crept back up them and positioned himself to the side of her door, where he had an excellent view of her opening her parcel.

Patti undid the Jiffy bag with such excitement that the stuffing from the parcel flew everywhere and the contents spilled out all over the ribbon-and-lace duvet. Patti looked at it. It wasn't at all how she had imagined from the picture. She picked up one of the items, a bunch of wools in green and pinks. And then she picked up the accompanying instructions.

'The work is designed to be done in a half cross stitch,' they intoned, and then in capital letters, after a brief line or two on how and where to knot her wool, it said 'DO NOT TRAMÉ'.

Patti frowned. Her dancing days had given her a quite comprehensive knowledge of French. She knew how to *plié, jeté,* even *sauté* (except that was more for cooking, but even so she knew it), but *tramé* was not something that she knew how to do. She picked up the tapestry itself. A nice picture of a garden and a gate, and some flowers and a pot, but it was all under threat, for to *tramé* it was quite obviously tantamount to building a motorway through it, but how could she not *tramé*, if she didn't know what it was?

'Oh *sugar,*' she said, and reached under her bed for the tin of unfinished apricots. Everything in her life seemed to be out of her reach, even the apricots. Elliott smiled and turned away from the door; not long before he'd be doing *that* for her.

'Heigh ho,' called Fulton from the hall. 'Mrs Dupont *arrive*.'

Mrs Dupont had indeed arrived. Her green quilted coat was still missing a button, unlike its owner, who never missed a thing.

'Such a dreary day,' she said loudly, as Fulton hung it carefully on an antler in the hall cupboard.

Elliott joined them, having arrived by the backstairs so as to remain undetected on his spying mission.

He always had a mad impulse to say 'Hullo, you old cow' whenever he saw Mrs Dupont afresh, rather like the insane desire to say something rude in church, just because you know you mustn't.

'All ready with the Ideas Book,' was what he actually said, and then they all went into the drawing room which was rife with his new style of wild-flower arrangements, all of which had suddenly decided to become heavy with earwigs.

'That's the trouble with hedgerow flowers,' said Mrs Dupont with satisfaction, 'they do attract the insects.'

'I haven't got long, I'm afraid,' said Fulton, which was what they had arranged for him to say, otherwise there would be no getting rid of 'our Jane', as they referred to the large woman.

'So what the Vicar and I thought,' continued Mrs Dupont, 'was an open-air barbecue to be held by the Ancient Monument. Drumsticks à l'Inde, Wiltshire Whoppers, that sort of thing. Yes?'

'I don't see why not,' said Fulton, bravely ignoring Elliott's raised eyebrows.

'Who are the sponsors this year?' asked Elliott, as the telephone rang and he went to answer it.

Mrs Dupont looked coy.

'I've had a lot of trouble, but I am thankful to tell you that we have now found one.'

Fulton tried to concentrate on Mrs Dupont, while listening intently to Elliott's conversation. He knew from Elliott's tone and the kind of answers he was giving that the caller must be the Countess. He also knew that she was busy telling him something that he, Elliott, did not want to know; and that being so it was obviously also going to be something that he, Fulton, would not want to know either.

'Wiltshire Whoppers.'

'I'm sorry?'

'Those are our sponsors – Wiltshire Whoppers.'

Elliott replaced the receiver carefully and then looked at his nails, a delaying habit of his that Fulton had not seen him do since they'd married Patti and moved to Flint House.

'Not bad news, I hope?' asked Mrs Dupont, meaning quite the opposite.

'No, not bad news. Not news at all, really.'

But Fulton noticed that he was a little pale, and so he hurried through the plans for the Charity Barbecue and wrapped up the meeting without even offering Jane Dupont, as she afterwards remarked bitterly to her friend Margaret Paine, 'even a thimble of sherry'.

'Well, what is it then?'

Fulton closed the front door behind Mrs Dupont, and they both returned to the drawing room, which to Elliott now appeared to be hopelessly overrun with earwigs and no longer the oasis of good taste it had seemed only a short hour ago.

'That was the Countess,' said Elliott.

'So I gathered,' said Fulton.

'With news,' said Elliott.

'Obviously,' said Fulton.

'Not good news,' said Elliott.

'No, well it wouldn't be, would it?'

Fulton tried to retain a philosophical look and sat down, crossing his legs carefully.

'She says,' said Elliott, 'she says—'

'Yes?'

'She says that – she says that that old drunk, Andrew Gillott Esquire – '

'The Honourable Andrew Gillott Esquire—'

'You can't be both—'

'Well, you know what I mean—'

'Anyway, continue.'

'She claims that he is claiming—'

'Yes.'

'To be the father of Patti's child.'

Fulton stared at Elliott. Every day that had passed over the last few months, days spent in happy chaos and merry anticipation, every day he had tried to think of all the bad things that might happen to destroy their peace and drive away the bluebird of happiness, because he had read somewhere that the misfortunes that occurred to people were always those of which they had not thought. And so he had thought and thought of all the terrible things that could happen to him, to all of them, but he had never once thought of this, that that dreadful friend of the Countess, he of the broken veins and the faded

42

cavalry twills, might have had, as the Vicar called it, 'carnal knowledge' with Patti.

'She couldn't.'

'Anything's possible with Patti.'

Elliott stared at the fireplace which was neatly stacked with logs.

'I feel sort of sick,' he said.

'I don't blame you.'

'I mean this changes *everything*.'

'Of course it does. I mean – of all the people in the whole world to be father to our baby.'

'Well, I know.'

'I'd even prefer the Vicar.'

'I don't think he can.'

'Of course he can't. He once hinted that it was something to do with his having had the mumps, but I think it's more to do with mum than mumps.'

'The point is, the point is she may not be right. I mean there's nothing to say that she *is* right, but—'

'Exactly, but. But just supposing it's true?'

'Exactly. A little Gillott in our midst.'

They both shuddered.

'Exactly. He'd make a beastly boy, and an appalling girl.'

'There's nothing for it, we'll just have to ask Patti.'

'She won't tell. Apparently it's against her principles.'

'She hasn't got any.'

'No, I know, but if she did have any, telling would be against them.'

'I wish she'd just tell me it's not true.'

'There's nothing for it but to wait and see.'

'See what?'

'See what it looks like. Or whom it looks like, rather.'

'Supposing it doesn't look like anyone?'

'Oh it will, babies always do.'

'What I mean is, supposing it doesn't look like someone, but only like anyone?'

'We'll threaten adoption.'

'All that sewing.'

Elliott looked hopelessly towards some crochet work in the corner.

'The Duc de Berry cradle.'

'Look, we mustn't panic. We must just carry on as normal, in our normal style. We must not let her know that we suspect a *thing*.'

'Yes, you're right.'

Elliott blew his nose quite suddenly.

'Now what?'

'Nothing. I just remembered how long it took me to make those first-size vests on very small needles.'

'Well don't.'

'No, you're right, I mustn't.'

'Pull yourself together. We must not upset Lady Tizzy. It's probably just one of that old tabby's *canards*.'

'Yes, the Countess can be a proper old witch when she wants.'

'I'll say.'

'Now, not a word. Patti must not suspect.'

But of course she did, for happiness, fragile as the cobwebs in her room that she would never allow to be dusted, was now something that she could no longer take for granted. Whereas before she daily expected Elliott to call her for her exercises, now she had to find him to ask him to join her. And Fulton, who loved her and patted her in a careless way, was now forever having to remember to do so.

She was too proud to ask either of them what it was that she had done (although she thought it *could* be the business of the tinned apricots), just as she was too proud to ask Elliott the meaning of the wretched word *tramé*. Instead she let their former contentment become something of the past to which she could look back, as to a delightful holiday.

'Do you remember when we made that crab apple jelly together? And Fulton found the hedgehog in the orchard and kept it in a box by the kitchen fire?'

Elliott put down his crochet work, which he was fast coming to loathe.

'Not down Memory Lane again, surely?' he asked, trying not to sound impatient.

'What do you mean?'

'Just now all you do is talk about the past.'

'Not surprising, really, I mean, is it?'

'Would you care to translate?'

'Yes, well, you know, not every mother makes it, not even nowadays. I mean Mr Benson—'

'Don't tell me, here comes one of Mr Benson's statistics. I don't think he's a gynaecologist at all, I think he's a walking encyclopedia.'

'Mr Benson says that if anything there is just as high a mortality rate, given the size of the population, *per capita*—'

'That means the same thing.'

'So? So what if it does? I know what I mean, and I think I'm going to die, and that's what I mean.'

Elliott stared at her. Somehow, probably because

they'd all been so busy, it had never occurred to him that Lady Tizzy might not make it.

'Last night I had a dream,' said Patti. 'I dreamed that I was going through this old garden gate and I saw Knightey, and he took me by the hand and told me to go with him, and I told him I couldn't, that I had to stay with the baby, but he made me leave it, and when I looked back – you were holding it.'

Patti's eyes were now filled with tears.

'Not that it matters because you'll make a much better mother than what I will,' she added.

Elliott put down his crochet work for the second time and went and sat beside her. Women did have premonitions when they were pregnant, he'd heard of it many times.

'Come on now, you're going to be all right,' he said.

'I don't think so,' said Patti. 'But whatever happens you promise you'll look after it?'

'You know I will,' said Elliott, just as Patti gave a little gasp.

'Oh flaming Ada, Ely-ot, would you Christmas Eve it, I've only started.'

'Oh flaming Ada, you only have, too.'

Elliott leaped to his feet and, with great presence of mind, rolled up the needlepoint rug.

'Now don't panic, just breathe while I get the car out. Remember what we've rehearsed? Nice little shallow breaths. In and out, that's right.'

He ran out into the drive, and then ran back in again for no better reason than that he hadn't felt so frightened since a wartime doodlebug hovered over their house at Bognor and his mother shut him in the larder.

46

Of course it had to happen while Fulton was out at a furniture sale, and it had to happen at five in the afternoon when the traffic through to Bath was at its busiest, and his car had only a teaspoon of petrol in its tank, and the wretched Benson was out delivering a calf.

'Is he a vet or a gynaecologist?' he heard himself shouting down the telephone to the secretary.

'It's a prize Friesian,' said the secretary. 'Mr Benson won a third at Smithfield last year.'

'Tell him I'll deliver the calf if he'll deliver the baby.'

'Mr Benson will be with her as soon as he can,' was the bored reply. 'Have you telephoned the ambulance?'

'Telephoned the ambulance? Do you know what you're saying? The ambulance takes an hour.'

He slammed down the telephone. There was nothing for it but to try driving her there on a hope and a prayer, or was it a wing? He settled the now yelling Patti into the back of his car.

'There, there, we'll be at the Clinic in no time,' he heard himself saying as he calmly tried to start the car with a Parker pen.

'There, there,' as they at last moved forward, to the accompaniment not of Patti's carefully rehearsed measured breaths but of wild cries of anguish.

First of all he thought he'd drive slowly so as not to precipitate the impending event, but then as the event seemed to grow less and less impending, and more and more immediate, he found himself putting his foot down and flying down the road, negotiating the traffic with the sort of reckless abandon usually only associated with hungry policemen returning home to their tea.

To his great relief it was not long before he was flagged down by such a person.

'Thank heavens for the boys in blue,' breathed Elliott, as Patti gave another piercing yell.

'Don't worry, sir, all part of the service since the cutbacks. Hop in.'

'I think Lady Tizzy's a bit beyond hopping,' said Elliott, who, now that help was at hand, was beginning to enjoy himself.

Blue light flashing, the police car raced to the Countryside Clinic with Elliott following at a more sedate pace. Sitting beside the policeman Patti stopped yelling, and smiled.

'You going to do all the delivering, then?' she asked.

'Don't think I can't.'

'Are you married, then?'

'No, not had the time, too busy delivering other people's babies.'

Patti gave a gasp as they negotiated the last corner to the Countryside Clinic.

'Sure you don't want to change your mind and have it out here? Be much cheaper.'

'Leave off, would you?' she gasped, as he held out his arm for her.

The policeman handed her over to the sister and then called after her, 'Still time to change your mind.'

Patti looked back at him for a second, and he at her.

'Fingers crossed?'

'You bet. And don't forget I'll be in to see Baby later on.'

'Was that your husband, dear?'

'No, no, he's at work.'

'And this gentleman?'

'He's—'

'Your husband—' said Elliott rushing up. 'And I insist on being there for the birth.'

He eyed the sister firmly.

'Very well,' said the sister. 'And who's this?'

Now Fulton too came rushing up.

'Oh him,' said Patti. 'He's me other husband.'


'How did you know what had happened?' asked Elliott some minutes later as they both sat waiting for the great event.

'It was pretty difficult,' admitted Fulton. 'I mean there I was with a van full of *fauteuils*—'

'Anything of interest?'

'Just one, a walnut *bergère* – anyway, there I was unloading the stuff into the stable when I noticed that the front door was open, the back door was open, your car had gone, Patti's suitcase had gone, and the needle-point rug in the drawing room was doing an imitation of a rolled-up newspaper—'

'So naturally you came to the quite proper conclusion that Patti and I had been practising a two-step for the Charity Barbecue when two masked marauders burst through the doors and kidnapped us?'

'Exactly. Shouldn't we be in there?'

'Of course we should, but I've got a feeling Sister doesn't want us.'

'Where's the wretched Benson?'

'Delivering a calf, of course.'

'I don't believe it.'

'Oh yes you do.'

'Oh yes I do.'

'I don't know what we're paying him for.'

Elliott looked at Fulton.

'Apparently it would help if Lady Tizzy was eligible for the Smithfield Show.'

'If this is Gillott's by-blow I have news for Mr Benson – I shall personally enter her.'

A small silence fell as Fulton's remark served to remind them both that there was still a question mark hanging over the whole proceedings.

'I've never really seen a newborn baby. I've only really seen them when they start looking like Winston Churchill and waving their plastic bottles about like cigars.'

'I've seen them on television in incubators.'

'Then they just look like jelly babies. I mean they don't look like their aunt's great grandmothers, or—'

'The Hon Andrew Gillott—'

'Now you promised not to say it out aloud ever again.'

The door from the delivery room opened, and one of the nurses popped her head out.

'Nearly there,' she said.

'Goody, goody. Is she behaving herself?'

'A whiff of pethidine, and they all behave themselves.'

'All those classes and breathing on the schoolroom floor, I don't know why I bothered,' said Elliott.

'Very useful if *you* ever decide to have a baby.'

'I'm only glad we decided not to go for the underwater method, if this is all that happens when you get to it.'

Fulton got up and started to walk up and down. At times of crisis it was his habit to try and remember various poems he had learnt as a child. Just now he was trying to remember Byron's 'The Swimmer'. At least he thought it was Byron's, although what sort of swimmer he had made with his bad foot, and when he had time for it between all the incest and the affairs, heaven alone knew. He was sure it began 'How many times have I—'

At that moment the door from the Labour Room, if that was what it was called, opened. Elliott, who had been sitting chewing a nail because in the rush he'd left his crochet at home, stood up. Fulton froze, as when playing statues. The nurse held a small bundle in her arms.

'At last,' breathed Elliott, and peered down into the blanket.

'Mr Featherstonhaugh?' asked the nurse innocently.

'Not lately,' said Fulton.

'Nor me,' said Elliott.

'Poor Mr Featherstonhaugh,' said Fulton, starting to laugh. 'I hope he knows what he's in for.'

'Don't laugh. It's not funny. Ours might look worse.'

They wandered down to the coffee machine, and having pressed a button for two black coffees and been sent two with milk and sugar, they wandered back again.

Another nurse emerged with another bundle.

'They're arriving thick and fast,' said Fulton.

'Not too thick, I hope and pray.'

'Lord Tisbury?'

'Yes,' they both answered, and without the smallest hesitation.

'You've got a lovely baby—'

The nurse looked down at the bundle in her arms and smiled, and then she looked up at them and smiled again.

'Not a poodle, *please*,' said Elliott.

The nurse placed the bundle in Fulton's arms.

'No, a beautiful baby girl, and she looks the image of her daddy.'

She smiled maternally up at Fulton.

'You'd have made a beautiful girl, Lord Tisbury, no doubt of that.'

'I can't believe it,' said Fulton, smiling down at the baby.

'Luckily, neither can I,' said Elliott.

# 3

The Honourable Mrs Gillott, ex-Mrs Aidan Parker-Jones, stared at her stationery, all of which bore the handle of which she had once been so proud – 'The Honourable'. Now it no longer gave her any satisfaction for she had found that Wiltshire was littered with titled persons of one kind or another. Being an Honourable, it had to be faced, was no longer a thrill. She ought to be a marchioness like her daughter Jennifer, or at least a baroness like the eccentric woman up the road, who only yesterday in Bedford's Delicatessen had recommended storing brown paper to wear as insulation against the Wiltshire winter. How she hated Andrew, her husband, for having three older brothers, all of whom appeared to be in robust health.

She also hated him for his own sake, and often found herself lying awake at night planning his demise. If he would only depart this life before she grew too old, she would be free to further her progress up the charts of Debrett's precedence list. Not only that, she could return to Kensington, which she longed for with the true passion known only to exiles. She longed to see a bus, or even her doctor's front door. In short, she longed for the days when she was her former self, before she allowed herself to be trapped into living in Wiltshire, a virtual recluse.

Naturally she had moved to Wiltshire for the best possible reasons: to draw Andrew away from the attractions of the Claremont Club, and to give their marriage the proper standing that only a house in Wiltshire and a small flat in town could give. It had been all right at first, because there had been so much to do, what with the furnishing of the house with practically undetectable reproduction furniture, and learning how to wear a hat to judge the 'Courgettes and Mixed Veg' class at the local fruit and flowers show; but after those thrills had died down, she found that life had slowed to a trickle of small events that would fail to thrill even the most deeply provincial (which having lived in Kensington she most definitely was not).

For who could look forward to a lecture on silk flower arrangements? Or a re-enactment of the Miracle of the Holy Roon in a tithe barn? These were not events to which one could wear one's newest Jason Jonet blouson and skirt. These were events organised for those whose idea of a social life was attending a barn dance with music provided by Billy Watkins and the Scramblers.

The trouble with life in the country, she had discovered, was that it went on. And on, and on, and on. It was life. Seasons changed, one flowing into another, seasons of mist and mellow fruitfulness followed by winter and more of the same, except fewer leaves. And then that was followed by the joy of being in England now that April was there, a poem that could only have been written by someone who was himself busy basking in the warmth of the Italian sun. And then after that came a very short spell known as 'summer in the country', when most sensible people went abroad, but not those who had settled in Wiltshire, who all despised 'abroad' and much preferred to stay at home and read leaflets on how to put in a pool with plastic liner for under ten thousand pounds, not counting the warm air heater and pool hoover, neither of which could be absolutely guaranteed to work, but which everyone agreed 'you had to have'.

Clarissa had insisted on putting in a pool this summer, because when, not if, she moved back to Kensington, she wanted to be able to leave the half-page advertisement in *Country Life* ('just too big for us finally') open on the table in the downstairs cloakroom, and it would be deeply unimpressive not to have the symbol of both a horse *and* a man diving into a wavy line beside it.

It was on rainy days, when she gazed into her walk-in cupboard with special illuminated glass shelves for her collection of beaded cashmeres, that she really became depressed. For not only did her Jason Jonet suits and her wrapped silk Karl Lagerfeld cocktail frocks remain resolutely unworn, but also her special country wear. It had been a shock, there was no denying it, but one of the worst aspects of the country was that it was quite unsuitable for 'country wear'. One could wear 'country wear' in town, and it could be, and was, very smart, but in the country one could only wear a succession of different varieties of thermal rainwear.

And as for getting one's hair done, well one might as well forget it, for the finger wave still lived and was practised in Wiltshire with the same devotion that nomads displayed when turning towards Mecca. A simple cut and blow dry left the recipient with an image of themselves normally only associated with photokit pictures issued by the police. Clarissa had now taken to wearing a series of wigs, which gave her added height, but which Andrew maintained made her look like a newsreader.

Andrew of course was no help, but then he never had been, really. Try as she could now, she simply couldn't understand why it was that she had taken it into her head to marry him. He was after all only an Honourable, and a penniless one at that. It had been the grief of losing dear Aidan, so suddenly and without warning. She had been so shocked at being left a widow so young and with a twenty-year-old daughter to bring up. She knew all this now, with the clarity of vision that a lifting of grief always brings, but *then* she had been numb, prey to the first man who came along and fell in love with her. If she hadn't been so distraught she would have had the sense to wait for something better. 'Never take the first bus that comes along,' Jennifer's old nanny used to say, and how right she was, how terribly, dreadfully right.

She had formulated some plans in her mind, but although they were all concerned simply, and solely, with escaping from Wiltshire and her exile there, they were not all of them, she had to admit, perhaps as practical as she would have liked. One of her 'plans' was to put weed-killer in Andrew's coffee every morning; it would be quite undetectable to him, but perhaps not quite so undetectable to a detective. Another idea was to spray his windscreen with some substance she had read about that brought on a massive coronary at high speed; but again therein lay a difficulty, that of procuring the substance. After all, it was not the sort of thing that could be bought over the haberdashery counter at Peter Jones, however comprehensive their range of goods. In fact, probably the best answer to her strong desire to return to the singularity of widowhood, and open her own emotional highway once again, was quite simply to commit a *crime passionnel* which the judge would treat with great sympathy once he heard the extent of her suffering.

For divorce, pure and simple, was simply not an alternative for Clarissa. There had never been a divorce in her family, and there had never been a divorce in Aidan's family, and she was certainly not proposing to make history by becoming the first person on either side to obtain one. Aidan may have only been City, and herself middle class, but their families still stood for something, even if all about them were throwing in the towel and dragging their names through the courts. No, even murder was preferable to that, she was happy to say.

All in all, the plan that had finally appealed most to her, and had also the purity of practicality, was that which she had come to call the Expedition. If she could only bring Andrew to realize that what his life lacked was a sense of adventure, and having brought him to this realiaztion, if she could only get him to turn his attention to going on some great trek to some far-flung place, there had to be a strong chance of losing him forever; for heaven knows, if he found it difficult to return on the last train back from London, then there had to be an equally strong chance of his not returning from somewhere more distant.

But, for some reason she simply could not understand,

ever since they had moved to Wiltshire, a sense of adventure was something that Andrew seemed to have left behind in a strong-box at his club. Not that he didn't go to London as often as she would permit him (he had had seventeen appointments with his dentist at the last count), but when not in London, he appeared to be quite happy pottering about in his motor car, going she knew not whither on one footling errand after another. Here was this former secretary of the Royal and Ancient Temple Society quite happy to potter about Wiltshire, when in the days before their marriage nothing less than a full range of mountains and some inaccessible plateaux could induce him to put a foot out of doors. It was maddening, and slightly repulsive.

Had Clarissa had any real interest she could have found out where Andrew went on his own in his motor car, and having found out she could only have rejoiced, for the truth was that the former secretary of the Royal and Ancient Temple Society was so bent on self-destruction that an observer could have been forgiven for thinking he was hell-bent on carrying out his wife's dearest wishes.

Having consumed his normal breakfast of bacon, egg and fried bread, followed by three Dunhill cigarettes, he would open his morning with a short tootle down the hill to the Lamb, which, having opened somewhat half-heartedly at ten-thirty to serve coffee to any tourists who had the misfortune to find themselves in the vicinity, needed little inducement to serve Andrew his 'pipe opener'. This was a seemingly innocuous beer served from a small bottle that had all the hidden power necessary to induce in him a feeling that there was life still around the person that he no longer recognised as being his mother's son. It was a darling of a confection, and after two or three, as he told the landlord in great confidence, 'a chap was able to focus on the *Life* without wanting to throw up all over the horse brasses'.

As a rule, the *Sporting Life* having been absorbed in enraptured silence, he would wobble to the telephone and reverse the charges to his long-suffering bookie, who had been persuaded to agree to this system on the understanding that Andrew would continue to lose as frequently as he had in the past.

This particular morning, as his wife stared at her personalised cards stacked neatly in the marblised desk set that held her stationery, Andrew's semi-mystical absorption of the runners in the Two-thirty at Goodwood was interrupted by the entrance of his old friend the Countess.

Just for a second Andrew hoped that she was a mirage, a side effect of the powerful beer, the second of which he had already broached; for not only did the Countess not frequent pubs, she had never been known to set one Rayne shoe inside them; and not only that, she didn't even live in Wiltshire, but in London and Sussex.

'Thought I'd find you here, you old fool,' she said happily, making it quite plain that she was not, after all, a mirage, but more a visiting camel to someone else's oasis.

'Good God,' said Andrew, and then panicking, 'I say, Clarissa's not with you, is she?'

'Now, do I look as if Clarissa's with me?'

Andrew thought for a minute. He wasn't quite

sure how someone looked if Clarissa was with them, but seeing that the Countess was looking remarkably chipper, despite her considerable age, he decided that she couldn't possibly have Clarissa in tow.

'What do you want?' He pointed at his glass.

'Not too early for a G and T, considering I've been up and doing since seven,' said the Countess, and she laid several brown folders importantly in front of her.

Andrew moved slowly towards the bar, and back again. He was fond of the old Countess, but not at this hour.

'Well,' said the Countess, accepting her gin and tonic without thanks, 'guess why I'm here?'

'Oh, I couldn't do that,' said Andrew with feeling, and making it sound as if it might be rude to do so.

'I'm moving,' announced the Countess. 'Thought you'd like to come and see some houses with me.'

'Oh no,' said Andrew, 'I did all that with Clarissa, and it was hell on wheels.'

'Nonsense,' said the Countess, 'you'll come with me to Stanton, and then we'll proceed from there.'

Andrew groaned, but the Countess looked at him the way she was wont to in the old days when he owed her too much money, even for her peace of mind.

'What's wrong with Sussex?' he begged. 'You've lived there all your life.'

'It's too old, and I'm getting too old to put up with the old.'

Andrew poured the rest of his beer into his glass. It was his third, but the Countess wouldn't know, and anyway if he was to spend the day with her he'd need more inner fuel than ever.

Entering the estate agents in Stanton with the Countess was not, he knew, going to be a spiritually uplifting experience, but, even so, he had not expected it to be quite so crucifying as it turned out. She treated the staff as if they were all Nubian slaves. She spoke to them sharply for no reason at all, and she returned every detail they proffered back to them, as if they had dealt her a marked card.

Andrew found his eyes wandering towards one of his currently favourite watering holes, the Red Lion. He could see that several more fortunate, unaccompanied gentlemen had already wandered in. He had a horrible feeling that it would be some time before he could find himself among the more fortunate inmates, particularly since, to everyone's numbed amazement, the Countess had suddenly found a property that she was pleased to think she might like to see round.

'And not too far from you either,' she told Andrew in a triumphant tone. 'I'll be able to keep an eye on you.'

Andrew stared at the brochure she was waving at him: a small eighteenth-century house surrounded by specially tinted, over-blue, estate agent's sky. The Countess was the reason he had married Clarissa; she was also the *force motif* behind moving Clarissa and himself to the country, on the understanding that Clarissa would hate it, and Andrew could divorce her for irreconcilable differences and return to his former happy existence at the Claremont Club. Neither of these two events had come to pass, but now a third one was about to happen, a consolidation of every nightmare: the Countess was going to come and live nearby, so he would not only have Clarissa keeping tabs on him, he would have Her

Ladyship as well. For fond as he was of the old girl (she was after all a great example of her kind), nevertheless she was still a complete pain in the backside, like most women.

'Oh, by the way, you know Lady Tizzy's had her brat, don't you?'

Andrew's heart lurched, as if the Countess was driving that particular organ, instead of her motor car.

'A girl. And you know I told Elliott it was yours?'

Andrew's gaze switched suddenly from a wistful contemplation, through the car window, of the now rapidly diminishing Red Lion. He stared at the Countess.

'What did you want to do that for?'

'Oh, I don't know, you know how it is – bored, I suppose.'

'But I mean to say, they could become most unpleasant.'

'No, no, Fulton's so delighted Mary says she's convinced that he thinks it's really his.'

'Lovely little woman, Lady Tizzy,' said Andrew, clutching the sides of his seat. 'Wonderful eyes.'

'She's as common as buttercups,' the Countess sniffed.

'Not to men she ain't,' said Andrew. 'There's not a man around who wouldn't walk on hot coals for Lady Tizzy.'

'Well, let's hope that whoever got his feet burnt last summer hasn't got too many distinguishing features,' said the Countess, driving down a one-way street and hooting loudly at the opposition.

'Really, people can be very boring.'

Andrew sat back and closed his eyes, as he normally did when the Countess was driving. If he could have, he would have raised a Dunhill to his lips and lit it, but he couldn't, because his hands were trembling, even more than was usual for him. He just didn't want to die before he'd had the early results from Goodwood.

'My dear, Georgiana is still with you?' asked Clarissa.

'Yes,' said Jennifer, trying to sound bored.

'*What* a long visit.'

'Yes, isn't it?' said Jennifer unhelpfully.

'Still, lots of time to talk over the old days.'

'Mmm.'

Jennifer rolled her eyes at Georgiana, who was sitting in the window seat staring out at a beautiful piece of planting for which she knew Pemberton was responsible. It was strange to think that all this could have been hers. If she hadn't run away from Pemberton after that first night they had spent together, she could be out there with him planning the new water garden; as it was, all she was planning at the present moment was how to tell Stranragh that she couldn't stay with him. She despised the idea of leaving a note on a chimneypiece, something that Jennifer had recommended. It seemed to lack proper courage. After all he had married her, he had paid her that compliment; the least she could do was to explain why she couldn't stay with him to him, in person. It was only polite.

'I would never tell a man something he wouldn't want to hear in *Scotland*,' said Jennifer, having replaced the telephone receiver. 'After all, up there, all alone, anything could happen.'

63

'Oh, I think I must,' said Georgiana. 'I think it's the only honourable thing to do.'

Jennifer made a little snorting noise before picking up her tapestry. Even though she didn't believe in such things, she could see that Georgiana was a masochist.

'Shall we go for a walk?' she suggested, because she was tired of doing the green bit at the bottom of her tapestry picture.

She looked out of the window, and seeing that Georgiana had been watching Pemberton in the garden, she quickly changed her mind and decided that a walk to the village would be more invigorating, because of the hill being so very beneficial to her tired muscles.

Of course it was not Georgiana's fault that Pember had come home early and interrupted their girlish idyll together, but now he was home, there was no sense in not taking proper precautions. 'No fish' was the reason Pember had given, the public reason; but nevertheless Jennifer had her suspicions. It was terribly dull of him of course, for Georgiana and she could not now talk openly together. Conversations happily begun in intimacy were now cut short abruptly to include Pember, who was usually too slow to understand, or if he did, seemed to disapprove.

'Women tell each other the oddest things,' he told Bloss. 'Things about men. Things a man would never dream of talking about. Most extraordinary.'

'My mother used to say two women in the house was the devil all over,' said Bloss.

'Your mother was right,' said Pemberton warmly. 'Get two women together and within a minute they're whispering behind your back, and hocking their jewellery, and the Lord knows what.'

'I shouldn't worry too much, m'lord. Lady Georgie's going soon,' said Bloss, just a little regretfully, because Lady Georgie's visit had been the first bit of excitement he had had since his lordship had been generous enough to present him with a Reliant Robin for three-wheeling down to the Queen's Arms.

'It's not that I want her to go, exactly,' said Pemberton. 'I just wish she wasn't staying.'

Seeing it was three minutes after six, Bloss poured them both their 'usual', and changed the conversation. For the past week the state of Lady Georgie's marriage had held him riveted. With the aid of a glass held against the morning room wall, he had been able to follow everything that was being talked about by her ladyship and her friend. Although the conversations had been somewhat less explicit than he could have wished, nevertheless they were riveting enough to make him grateful that he was blessed with good hearing.

'I used to take her out you know. Lady Georgie,' said Pemberton after a short silence. 'She was rather keen on me,' he added.

Bloss murmured appreciatively. He was only too keen to hear more, but he knew it would be fatal to look interested, so he picked up a pair of grape scissors and started to polish them.

'I suppose, I suppose you could say that she threw herself at me, really. But on the other hand, one does have to remember that she was only nineteen, and I was – I was more mature.'

'Well, you would have been,' said Bloss.

'It was very difficult for me, because there were so many in those days. Beautiful girls all of them too, and I mean, it wasn't as if I was even a photographer, or a film director. Of course, with someone like Lady Georgie, one was aware of the deep responsibilities. I mean she's a sensitive little thing. But you know how it is, Bloss, if the gods keep proffering you fruit for the picking, let's face it, is it up to one to refuse?'

Bloss now felt it was incumbent on him to make a reply of some sort.

'A gentleman of his lordship's looks will always have temptations,' he said, neatly replacing the grape scissors in their leather box. 'Always, even now.'

'Yes, being handsome and rich has great responsibilities,' agreed Pemberton. 'That's why I married my wife. I felt she had a reliability about her. Not so good looking that she would always be pushing off with the, but – well, you know what I mean, and at the same time I felt she knew what I would need. Sons, a home, that sort of thing. I just wish she was more interested in sex, but then they do say women go off that sort of thing after babies, don't they?'

Bloss held up a decanter.

'Another one before you change, m'lord?'

'Thank you. By the way, what am I changing for?'

'You're presenting the Women's Guild Cup to the lady who picked the most soft fruit for the Women's Guild Market.'

'Am I? Can't Jennifer, can't her ladyship do that?' said Pemberton, appalled.

'No, they wanted your lordship.'

'I suppose her ladyship said that. If you ask me, it's

just another way of getting me out of the house so that she and Lady Georgie can go on gossiping. I tell you, Bloss, your mother was right.'

From the main hall they could hear Jennifer calling. Pember raised a finger to his lips. Bloss nodded, and opened a door that would lead his lordship safely out of the butler's pantry and through the old servants' hall to the garden.

'God bless you, Bloss,' said Pemberton, as he crept away.

Jennifer flung open the door of the butler's pantry a very short minute later, but not so short that Bloss was not able to magic their glasses away and pop a mint in his mouth before facing her ladyship in full sail.

'What are you doing crouching in here sucking mints, Bloss?' Jennifer demanded, because Bloss always got on her nerves, and never more than when he put on his innocent act.

'Silver,' said Bloss with difficulty, because the mint was a large one with a soft centre, and he didn't want to spoil it by biting into it too soon.

'Where's his lordship?'

'I don't know, said Bloss truthfully.

'No, nor do I, and now it seems I'll have to go and present this wretched cup to the Women's Guild, since he has, as usual, not seen fit to remember. It'll quite spoil Lady Georgiana's last evening with us. I'm quite cross, Bloss.'

'Yes, well you would be,' said Bloss.

'Yes, I am. Are you sure you haven't seen him?'

'Quite,' said Bloss, suddenly noticing that the old Russian samovar needed a polish. 'Yes, m'lady, quite.'

Jennifer made a disbelieving noise and went out without closing the door, as if she wanted to be able to see into the butler's pantry at all times, as if she couldn't believe that his lordship wasn't going suddenly to materialise in the middle of the dusters and the long-term silver polish. Bloss bit into his mint and slowly chewed on the soft centre. If things went on as they were, with luck he would soon be getting a Ford Fiesta to replace the Reliant Robin.

Jennifer paused, frowning, in the middle of the hall. Things were not working out as they should be. And now there was the unmistakeable sound of a car stopping in the middle of the drive. She walked to the window. She hated unexpected visitors, even though she had a large staff, and Bloss to open the door. It took her back to her childhood, and all those hateful occasions when her mother would push her about drawing rooms using her as a miniature maid, and as a prop for her beauty, for she had been a plain child.

'Any problems, your ladyship?'

Bloss appeared, still chewing on his mint.

'Several,' said Jennifer, as she went to open the door because Bloss still had his silver-cleaning apron on.

'We just had to come and see you, because we were so near,' said the Countess, trying not to pant as she reached the last step of the long flight of stone steps that led to the great doors.

'Yes,' said Andrew, grinding a cigarette into the eighteenth-century stone with the edge of a run-down heel. 'Had to come and see you.'

'How very sweet of you,' said Jennifer, and she and the Countess kissed the air either side of each other's heads. 'Very sweet. Guess who's here?'

'Pemberton?' asked Andrew hopefully.

'Georgiana,' said Jennifer. 'But she's going tomorrow.'

'I didn't know she was here,' said the Countess, sounding a little indignant.

'Well, you wouldn't, would you?' said Andrew. 'You're usually in Sussex.'

'Even so, it would have been nice.'

'She's usually in Sussex,' said Andrew again, but this time to Bloss, who had now found a jacket and was holding the door.

'Very nice too, Sussex,' said Bloss.

'Too many less than Admirables,' said the Countess. 'They're always lowering their flags, and running tight ships, and boring everyone to tears.'

'Careful now. Bloss was in the navy, as I remember it.'

'Not as such,' said Bloss modestly, and opened the drawing room door for the party to proceed thankfully towards Pemberton's lavish supply of beverages.

'What will you all have?' asked Jennifer.

'Champagne, because I'm feeling I should celebrate,' said the Countess. 'Good gracious, Georgiana.'

She moved towards Georgiana, who had been sitting quietly by the fire imagining the moment she would tell Stranragh of her intention to leave him.

'You look frightful,' said the Countess, kissing the air, this time either side of Georgiana's head.

'I feel fine,' said Georgiana.

'You look terrible,' said the Countess. 'You look like a charity poster.'

Andrew looked down at Georgiana.

'She's right, you know, you do look frightful,' he told her.

'I feel fine,' said Georgiana again.

'You'll have some champagne, won't you?' Jennifer asked Georgiana, who didn't reply.

'Where's Pemberton?' asked the Countess.

She sat down and everyone else followed suit, a little as if she were royalty.

'I only wish I knew,' said Jennifer. 'He's meant to be presenting the Soft Fruit Cup to the Women's Guild, but he can't be found.'

'What a to-do,' said the Countess to no-one in particular.

'I'll have a Scotch and soda – the usual,' Andrew told Bloss.

Bloss nodded. He knew Mr Gillott's 'usual'.

There was a short pause during which Jennifer wondered if Pemberton had, after all, done his duty and gone to present the Soft Fruit Cup, and Andrew offered Georgiana a cigarette in a rather hopeless kind of way, as if he knew very well she didn't smoke but couldn't think of anything else do do.

'I have found a house to live in,' said the Countess to the room at large, and in the manner of a person who had been previously homeless, and not the owner of three other properties.

'How lovely,' said Jennifer. 'Anywhere we know?'

'No, it's hardly on the market, but it's not far. Must be near friends.'

'But you don't like your friends,' Andrew complained.

'No-one likes their friends, that is why they live near them.'

There was a short pause while everyone tried to work out what she meant.

'The house is of the right age,' went on the Countess.

Here at least everyone felt easy. There was only one age – the eighteenth century.

'It needs a great deal doing to it. But the garden is not too big.'

'Sounds fun,' said Georgiana, still seated in a remote corner of the fireplace.

The Countess ignored her. She not only ignored her, she continued to speak, raising her voice slightly, as if to signal to the rest of the company that she considered that what her niece thought, or felt, was of no interest to anyone, least of all her ladyship. This did not go unobserved, as it was meant not to, for there was no-one there so unversed in such nuance that they could not pick up a signal of such significance. Nor was Georgiana able to ignore it, for Georgiana, by both her unhappy appearance and her presence in Jennifer's house, was an embarrassment. No newly-wed girl, everyone knew, should look as she did, particularly not when it was the Countess herself who had helped to arrange the marriage of Lady Georgiana Longborough to the Third Baron Stranragh. Georgiana was a speaking criticism of her aunt's abilities to arrange life in its proper social order.

Georgiana looked helplessly into the fireplace, which was sporting an over-large dried-flower arrangement in a copper pan. Bloss, who for reasons of his own had not left the drawing room, moved quietly forward and refilled her glass. Georgiana looked at him gratefully. Bloss felt sorry for her, and she knew it. He looked into her large grey-blue eyes and thought how beautiful they were, and what an old cat the Countess was being. She quite touched his heart, like one of the portraits in the Wallace Collection, a postcard of which he kept in the corner of his mirror. Say what they would about Lady Georgie, and this was just the start, she was a true aristocrat, he thought, same as what his lordship was, and like his lordship, she knew her place. The same, alas, could not be said for her ladyship, who, try as she might, and heaven knows she had, would always remain an also-ran, lacking that indefinable style that only a thousand years of breeding could bring.

Andrew slipped away from the drawing room just as the Countess was taking the assembled company through the drawing room of her future home, and out on to the terrace. His escape was motivated less by a warm desire to find his old friend Pemberton and more by a deeper desire to find out the result of the last race at Goodwood.

Knowing Pemberton as he had from boyhood, he had no trouble in searching him out, for there was only one place where a chap like Pemberton could be found, and that was not in the nursery suite with his children, but in the stables with his dogs and horses, hobnobbing with a couple of the lads.

'No-one else knows I'm here, do they?' asked Pemberton without even greeting him.

'Not really, no,' said Andrew, going to the stable telephone to contact the racing services.

'What do you mean?'

'Only,' said Andrew, dialling with a nicotine-stained finger, 'only that if they thought it they would have come by now, but since they haven't, they obviously won't.'

Pemberton contemplated this statement, and finding

it satisfactorily lacking in any threat to the present harmony, went back to the tack room where one of the lads was celebrating his birthday with bevvies handed round in paper cups.

'I don't know what it is,' said Andrew, joining them a minute later to celebrate backing the winner of the last race, 'but everything's so much more fun when there are no women around.'

'That goes without saying,' said Pemberton, and he looked sombrely into the middle distance, as if in his mind's eye he could see a future peopled only by female persons, and an equal number of future events that would be ruined by them.

'They're a hell of a thing, but there you are, you can't do without them, not if, as I did, you want an heir to the whole thing.'

'Yes, I've been blessed with luck on that one,' Andrew agreed. 'No family obligations. No real reason to get married.'

'Yes, but you did.'

'Yes, I did, but only because of being in the unhappy position of not having enough dibs to even rob Peter to pay Paul. I was robbing Peter and Paul, and so there was no way out. It was either the Mu-Mu maiden, or nothing.'

'Can never remember why you call Clarissa that!'

Andrew groaned loudly, as if the very memory of his present wife caused him intolerable pain.

'First time – she – you know. Next morning she was wearing this frightful garment, and when I asked her what she was sporting, she said a "mu-mu". Can you imagine?'

Pemberton looked at him sympathetically.

73

'Must have been terrible.'

'Terrible, it was frightful. I burned the thing when we came down here.'

'Well done.'

'Not so "well done". She only went out and bought another one. Even worse.'

'Jennifer's got some pretty fearful garments, but nothing with a name like that, thank heavens.'

'No, well, Jennifer's not such a bad egg. It's her mother that ought to be put down.'

Pemberton left Andrew to collar one of his favourite bottles which he kept behind the tins of linseed and hoof oil in the tack-room cupboard. When he returned they trotted off together in the direction of the feed room, and ensconced themselves happily on a number of straw bales that had been tucked in a corner for that particular purpose. 'His Lordship's throne', it was known as round the yard.

'This is the life,' said Pemberton. 'I'm very glad you turned up. I get a bit lonely sometimes, you know. Not that Bloss isn't a stalwart, but you always make me feel better. I think it's because you're usually so miserable.'

'Yes, that stands to reason,' Andrew agreed. 'Nothing pulls *me* down so much as some other fellow's good fortune. Speaking of which – have you seen Georgiana?'

'Looks frightful, doesn't she?'

'And she's only been married a few months.'

'To me she looks as if she's got something you know – terminal.'

'Oh, I don't know, nowadays not even marriage need be terminal. Things have come on a bit.'

'I meant non-operable.'

'Yes, I know what you meant. By the way, have you heard about our Lady Tizzy?'

'Why? Has she foaled?'

'How did you know?'

'Oh I knew she was in foal, Jennifer told me.'

Pemberton cleared his throat, and then whistled silently.

'You know, you know what the Countess told Fulton?'

Andrew started to laugh.

'No,' said Pemberton with caution.

'She only went and told him, she only went and told him she thought I was the father of the – that it was mine.'

'Damn cheek,' said Pemberton. 'As if she'd fancy you. She's got more taste.'

'Hang on, I'm not that bad.'

'Lady Tizzy's a beautiful woman, and a lovely soft, sweet creature,' said Pemberton. 'How on earth could anyone think – as if she would.'

Both men stared at each other and unbeknown to each other simultaneously recalled the excitements of the previous summer when Lady Tizzy had strolled artlessly into their lives, making their existences both more exciting and more tolerable.

Andrew lit a cigarette.

'Who do you think is the father?'

'Someone of distinction. After all, Gerard Tisbury was not no-one, was he? I mean she's used to being with a gentleman. Someone of position, I would have thought.'

'I think it was that chap who came to help with the gardening, just after Sir G snuffed it. You know, the tall

75

one with the plait and the blond streaks. The one who always had his shirt off.'

'No, it wasn't him.'

'I saw her looking at him a lot.'

'I look at my gardener, but it doesn't mean I want to go to bed with him.'

'Well, whoever it is, he's got a baby daughter.'

'A filly, eh?'

'Yes, a filly.'

Pemberton leant forward for the bottle and topped up both their glasses.

'A filly,' he said dreamily.

Andrew raised his paper cup.

'To little Miss—'

'To little Miss—'

They both looked at each other and started to laugh.

'What *will* she be called?' asked Pemberton.

'Miss Montrose-Benedict-Cavanagh.'

'I don't know where they get these names *from*,' said Pemberton.

'Whatever, she's sure to be a cracker.'

'Yes, she is, isn't she?'

And so saying, they both raised their glasses in a toast.

# 4

Quails was a fashionable London hairdressers, but
not so modish or fashionable that a client such as Lady
Mary Lawton was likely to be disturbed by the sudden
entrance of a pop star, or the outlandish behaviour of a
photographic model anxious for attention. There was no
doubt that for its clients this was one of Quails' chief
attractions. Its tranquil atmosphere was such that a
person such as Lady Mary was able to have a shampoo
and set twice weekly, and still enjoy a feeling that
she was in a home from home. There were, however,
some small excitements which, it had to be admitted,
Quails could offer, and home could not. Once a minor
member of Royalty (Lady Mary abhorred the new
fashion for calling them Royals) threw a bottle of nail
varnish at Rosa the manicurist, and on another occasion
two ladies who were both involved with the same
gentleman (though neither married to him) had to be
hastily placed on different floors before, as Arturo,
the affable owner, put it, 'there was an explosion';
but generally speaking the atmosphere in Quails was
that of an eighteenth-century salon. Clients gossiped
gently, worried about whether to have their ends done,
read magazines, drank their coffee, and wrote letters to
their lovers in the reasonable hope that life was, for
the most part, something that could be faced (always

77

provided, of course, that they had had a shampoo, set and manicure).

This particular morning Lady Mary, while awaiting Arturo's comforting attentions, was following the impassioned outpourings (in violet ink on bright blue paper) of the lady sitting next to her. Her 'own one', it appeared, had not even had the decency to leave her for another, but was, it seemed, absenting himself from her life as a 'matter of principal'. The writer could not understand this, but then, as Lady Mary reflected, people who write on bright blue paper in violet ink very rarely do understand a devotion to principles. Sometimes, as in this case, they can't even spell them.

It seemed that she had had nights of love with her 'own one' such as she had never known with another. Theirs had been a rapture even he would surely miss? Had he no feelings?

Mary shifted her gaze back to the *Tatler* as her neighbour took a fresh piece of follow-on paper. It was strange how passion boiled beneath the most surprising façades. To look at the woman currently unleashing her emotions on the thick sheets of correspondence, you would have thought that she was an average lady of conservative disposition whose idea of passion was reading a Georgette Heyer novel on the train back to Pewsey. But such was not, quite obviously, the case. Hidden beneath her neighbour's double-ply cashmere jumper and matching navy blue gaberdine skirt was someone who was prepared to go to any lengths to continue making a fool of herself. It seemed now, on page five, that the silly woman could even contemplate suicide rather than face life without her 'own one'.

Mary sighed a smallish sort of sigh. She would have liked to shake the silly woman. No doubt her 'own one' was a worthless sort of person, and her nights of passion with him grotesquely incongruous. It was somehow absurd to think of this woman with her outward respectability embroiled in some degrading affair. As if one had walked through a door in Carlton House Terrace to be greeted by Madame Sin and her band of girlies. 'Unsuitable' was the word, and one which her mother, the Countess, employed a great deal; but, nonetheless, it was suitable on this occasion. No doubt it would be a comfort to her to know that, if she did commit suicide, her hair would be looking lovely.

'You're going to the Ball.'

Arturo made this a statement, for they both knew that Lady Mary would never miss an opportunity to support the Friends of the Ancient Monuments Society. Old buildings were one of her favourite causes, because the people who loved old buildings were the best at organising charity events. There was no particular reason for this, but it was always so. The Ancient Monuments Society always held their balls and soirées in one or other of their newly restored buildings, and there was nearly always a theme and costumes required; much more fun than political fund-raising or those frightful bashes in aid of child cruelty.

Arturo held up the ostrich feather that Lady Mary had handed to him. He placed it temporarily on one side of her head, and then equally temporarily on the other side of her head, for they both knew that sooner or later he would place it at the back, in the coil of beautiful dark hair that he was about to loop into a style 'à la

'Pompadour', to go with her pale yellow dress with muslin panniers that she had been kindly lent for the occasion.

'I couldn't face a wig,' said Mary.

'Too hot,' agreed Arturo.

'And sometimes they make it difficult to be oneself.'

Arturo nodded appreciatively. Lady Mary was beautiful and aristocratic, and must always be 'herself', they both knew that. He was devoted to her. Not because she was a regular client, for he had many of those that he would willingly never see again, but because she was as charming as she was beautiful. Never once did she show impatience. Never once did those beautiful strange unmatching eyes of hers betray anything but a very English calm. She was the epitome of everything that the continental nature admired, and abhorred, in the English. If someone trod on her foot she would never betray pain. If they over-charged her, she would never complain. If a fire broke out in the salon, she would remain calm, as she was now doing when he pulled her hair too sharply.

And then too she had an unusual side to her nature, for, as everyone knew, she shared her life with not one man but two, and, in the Venetian style, they all attended the major society events of the year together. It was very interesting to think of her being so accommodating, so calmly accommodating. There was an Italian expression for it, which, happily perhaps, was untranslatable.

Mary watched Arturo winding her hair around his hand. She had every confidence in his artistry, for there was little doubt that he was artistic. Although Hugo and Lucius both denied that either hairdressers or photographers could be artists in the true sense of the word, nevertheless there was something very special about the way Arturo could cut, dress and arrange hair. If it was not 'artistic', it was no exaggeration to say it had 'artistry'.

Tired now of watching her own image, Mary lifted yet another copy of the *Tatler* and held it up to read. She would look quite passable tonight, of that there was no doubt (passable had been her parents' highest compliment). The copy of the *Tatler* was an old one, but nevertheless interesting, because it was one that she had, it seemed, missed. She must have been on Capri, where she still owned a small property. Or perhaps she had been staying with friends in Sardinia; for whatever reason, it was not a copy that she had seen, which was strange in itself, for it contained Georgiana's wedding pictures. Mary stared at them as if they were likenesses from some previous decade.

Georgiana wearing a tiara that had been kindly loaned to her by her mother. Her mother and father seated in the wedding group wearing the studied expressions of people who were hoping that their daughter was now 'settled', and nothing more sensational than a christening would now occur to either her, or them, and they could return to living a life that was poised between the library and the stables. Of course, had the photographer been from *Horse and Hound* they would have been smiling, but since he quite clearly wasn't, they weren't. Mary did not like Georgiana's parents, not just because they had, in her opinion, neglected Georgiana, but because they were old-fashioned in the wrong kind of way and did not approve of the sort of people that Mary liked. It had been no thanks to them that Georgiana had been finally and safely married off to James Stranragh, although to have watched their smug, establishment airs at the wedding, one would have thought they had worked tirelessly for their daughter's future, and that her happiness had been their only aim in life. Instead of which, it had been left to the rest of the family to rally round and give her some sort of 'background'.

Arturo took a step back. Mary lowered the *Tatler*. He raised the back mirror. Mary turned her head. It was elevating to see what charming effects others would see at the back of her head tonight.

'Charming, Arturo, thank you.'

Mary shut the copy of the *Tatler* and stood up.

'Thank you,' she said again.

Arturo inclined his head. He was very pleased.

Mary looked down at the closed magazine. Georgiana had gone from her life. Buried with Stranragh in Scotland. She would write to her some time soon, and she would find out why it was that they never came to London. Why had she not seen her cousin? However virile her husband, she would write to Georgiana, and she thought out the phrase carefully as she tipped the boy with the earring who had shampooed her hair; however virile, the honeymoon must surely be over now? As the receptionist held out her coat, Mary mentally added one exclamation mark, just one to this phrase, and then she walked out into the street and hailed a taxi. Soon she would be home. Hugo would be making some lemon tea, Lucius would have just finished putting a full stop on a page of his newest, and vaguest, novel (entitled *The Quest*). Bach would be playing on every floor, and there would be a strong smell of their favourite room scent, the all-pervasive Stephanotis. At this moment her life was, without any doubt, quite passable.

If James Stranragh's virility had once been in question, it was no longer. And certainly not to his wife. Too late, far too late, she had realised that her old friend's advice had been sensible. She should have left a note upon the chimneypiece in the library, just as her mother or her grandmother would have done. Then he would not have been able to do as he had done.

Yesterday he had come to her room and ordered her to get up. Standing by the door, as if he was afraid that she might have something catching, he had ordered her to get up.

'I've tried, but I can't.'

'Pull yourself together.'

She pushed back the bedclothes and tried to stand, but then the familiar black crowded into her eyes and the room began to disappear, and he had been forced to help her back to bed. He had left her alone. The rain, usually so comforting when you were in bed, drizzled and grizzled against the high windows, and the wind made the noise of a child crying monotonously. Boarding school crying, a long unvaried sound that held one note.

After that visit he kept away from her room as if, now, he was convinced that she had something contagious. Once he sent someone to ask her if she wanted anything to eat or drink, but she had only asked for more bottled water. She slept unceasingly, and for the little time that she was awake she wondered how it was that she had thought it a good idea to come back.

'You asked for it, then,' Nanny would say, whenever she related some story of being bullied at school. 'I'm sure you asked for it. You're very contrary, and contrary people always ask for it.'

She had, she knew, asked for it this time too, and rather more than ever.

It had been her own stupidity and pride at 'doing the right thing' that had brought her back to Scotland, just as it was Stranragh's pride that had made him do as he had done. She hated him, and yet she couldn't blame him. After all it was her fault that they had married. She had married him, he had not married her, and so she had no-one to blame but herself.

With a vague attempt at humour she realized that there were many women who liked 'that sort of thing'. Unfortunately she was not one of them. Her childhood had robbed her of any fascination with physical violence. Perhaps because her parents had never had a son, they had not seen fit to spare the rod with her. It was unusual, but in her case she had been privileged to be treated as a boy. And Nanny, too, was allowed free rein to make up for her disappointment at Georgiana not having been a member of the male sex.

Before she had come back to Scotland, she had had quite precise plans about her future. She would return to London, find herself an occupation, and James would divorce her. It had all seemed quite easy when she had been with Jennifer; they had discussed the future in an optimistic, feminine way which allowed for nothing but the best possible co-operation from James. They assumed that since he couldn't be a man, he would obviously now be a gentleman, because that is what they had been brought up to assume. Only at the last did Georgiana doubt the wisdom of returning to Scotland. With the kind of pragmatic second sight that was typical of her, she had thought it better to choose neutral ground to tell Stranragh.

He might 'do' something was her final vague reasoning. Well, he had 'done' something, and it was too late to bemoan her eternal stupidity.

Georgiana was sleeping curled up in the embryonic misery to which, in childhood, she had so often been reduced, when Dr McCulloch awoke her.

'Lady Stranragh?'

Georgiana awakened, looked at him briefly, and then closed her eyes again.

'Lady Stranragh? It's Doctor McCulloch.'

She could hear a chair being placed beside her bed and breathing such as a man has who is a smoker. Then she felt a hand placed on her forehead, rough, but thankfully cold. It smelt of nicotine. Georgiana moved away from it, but opened her eyes.

Dr McCulloch sat on her bedroom chair, upright and moustached. He stared at her.

'How do you feel?'

Georgiana turned her head away.

'Not very well.'

'Can you tell me any symptoms you think you might have?'

'I—'

Georgiana closed her eyes again.

'Have you had some sort of fall?'

'I think I might have.'

There was a long silence.

'Lady Stranragh, your husband is concerned about you.'

'Did he tell you that?'

'Not in so many words, but I don't imagine he would have telephoned me otherwise, do you?'

'I have no idea.'

'Lady Stranragh, would you mind if I examined you?'

'Yes, very much.'

'Is there any particular reason why you don't want me to examine you?'

'Yes. I feel too ill.'

'You have bruises?'

'A few. Not really.'

'From this "fall" perhaps?'

'Perhaps.'

To give himself a little time Dr McCulloch took out a thermometer and placed it in Georgiana's mouth. She looked at him dully. She didn't like doctors.

'You know, it never ceases to surprise me how many of my women patients injure themselves "falling over". It seems that members of your sex are more than a little careless, Lady Stranragh.'

He removed the thermometer from Georgiana's mouth. Not surprisingly her temperature was sub-normal, to the point where it could be said to be abnormally so.

'I think I might have to send you to hospital.'

'Oh, I don't think so.'

'Lady Stranragh,' Dr McCulloch sounded impatient, 'how often does your husband beat you?'

Georgiana sat up a little.

'My husband doesn't "beat" me, Doctor McCulloch,

my husband has never beaten me. My husband raped me, and that, as you know, is a legal impossibility.'

Dr McCulloch stared at her.

'Nevertheless, not very pleasant.'

Georgiana lay down as Dr McCulloch stood up.

'I can't say I'm not worried about you, Lady Stranragh. Very worried.'

He looked down at her. She was in a bad state of shock, and it would not take a genius to diagnose that. If he didn't suspect that she might also be suicidal, he would have left her some pills to tranquillize her, but, as it was, he felt it would be better to leave her nothing. She was obviously, when she was well, quite a beautiful little creature. He would like to have said many things to her husband, but he knew that, as always in such cases, it would do very little good, very little good at all.

'I shall come back tomorrow.'

She opened her eyes again as he reached the bedroom door.

'Doctor McCulloch—'

He waited for the inevitable plea.

'My husband—'

'I'll not say a word, Lady Stranragh.'

She closed her eyes again. For a second it seemed to Dr McCulloch that her face was whiter than the pillows upon which it lay, but that was possibly only because of the bruising.

He sighed as he closed the door quietly. In his young days, doctoring in Glasgow, it had always been 'Oh, Doctor McCulloch – not a word to my husband, mind?' But hearing those same words said here, was somehow more shocking to him. Either that or he was growing old and sentimental, for to think of a little thing like that being knocked about turned his stomach over.

He paused on the stairs and gazed out on to the parkland below. He would love to think that Lady Stranragh was a spoilt Society darling who had asked for, and received, everything that she deserved. Back in his Glasgow days, before a distaste for cities and people pulled him back to the countryside, he would have been content with the comfort of such a cliché, but now it was no longer possible. Women were unfathomable when it came to men, that at least he had learnt. The first baby he had delivered, on a bed set in the middle of a single living room where they ate and slept, had been to a woman whose husband lay beside her all the while in a drunken stupor. And not a murmur did she make, nor a groan, for all the pain she felt, for she would not have him disturbed. Why? Perhaps for the same reason that that poor girl lay upstairs in the condition that she was in.

Lord Stranragh was waiting for him in the library, by prearrangement. He found it easier not to look him in the eye. But because he was, he knew, the only doctor for miles, he was able to address him with a remarkable lack of respect, something which he dearly hoped his lordship would not fail to notice. And then he left him with a promise to return the following day. As always in these cases, he couldn't help feeling a sense of bewilderment, for to look at the man and to hear him talk you wouldn't have thought him capable of cuffing a dog.

\* \* \*

'I don't like the iron tablets, they make my teeth look black.'

Dr McCulloch had been coming to see Georgiana for some weeks now.

'If vanity's rearing its ugly head, then we must be feeling better.'

He put a thermometer in Georgiana's mouth, even though they were both well aware that it was only a ritual and the fact that it was permanently subnormal an irrelevance to both of them.

'One day you'll reward me with a nice ninety-eight point four.'

Georgiana smiled slightly. This was another part of their now daily routine. He liked to sigh and grieve over her lack of progress, or her sub-normal temperature, or her low blood pressure.

'What shall we talk about today, now?'

'The same as yesterday?' she suggested hopefully.

'If you want to.'

'You were telling me about the old tramp, and your mother and your aunt wanted to help him, remember?'

'Was that it, now? Aye, yes, maybe it was. Well, now, if you remember, Charlie used to come up to the house about once a month, and his clothes were always in an awful state. Dreadful. And the smell was something terrible. And my mother used to say to my father after each visit—'

Georgiana slid down the bed a little, still watching Dr McCulloch. He continued with the story, all the time observing any little improvements that she might show. That she was taking an interest in his stories was good, no more of that endless sleeping. Her eyes were a little brighter, and her nails a little pinker, and there was now no need to awaken her when he arrived. Even if he could not get her to eat, he could now at least get her to smile. It was something, but it was not enough. He had hoped for slightly more, but was, for the moment, content to let time and patience lull her back into a renewed interest in life. Of course, had he been a city doctor he would have treated her quite differently. He would have given her a course of tranquillisers to run concurrently with a course of sleeping tablets, and if they hadn't kept her quiet enough he'd have had her admitted to a private clinic where they would have amused themselves by reducing her to a state of insensibility and further drug dependence; and all this in exchange for more money than a man could dream of.

'And so my father turned to my mother and said "That was very good of you, dear, but you must know that it will be another twenty years before Charlie changes *those* clothes too." '

Georgiana smiled.

'I'd have loved to have seen him when he came out of the stables, after you'd bathed him and scrubbed him. Was he really quite white?'

'Ach, he was as white as driven snow until his neck and his face, which made him look like a skewbald pony.'

Georgiana stared past the doctor.

'You make Scotland seem quite different.'

'Aye, well I would, wouldn't I?'

Dr McCulloch never smiled, but as he left he touched the top of her head. At first she'd seemed embarrassed when he did this, but after a few days she appeared to accept it, in the same way that she appeared to accept his calling her by her Christian name.

'Goodbye now.'

Dr McCulloch's heavy footfall down the three little stairs from her bedroom signalled the end of Georgiana's afternoon, and the start of yet another whole day until he returned. She stared up at the ceiling. It had been some time since James had come to visit her, which was probably why she had been feeling better. Sometimes, in the night, she thought she heard him outside her bedroom door, and it frightened her; and sometimes she thought she could sense him outside in the grounds, walking about, perhaps staring up at her window. Wherever he was, she imagined he must now hate her as much as she hated him.

'Georgiana?'

She had been back in bed for an hour or two, half-dozing, half-dreaming, little images from her life appearing in patches, small pieces of unmatched mosaic. The highly polished floors at school that always smelled of coffee from the dried grounds that they swept over them. The large lumps of stale bread that Nanny gave you for tea. Kaminski, her first lover, watching her in the taxi the night she ran away from Mary's house and went to live with him.

'Georgiana?'

It was James. Georgiana stared across at the door. There was no telephone in the bedroom, and even if there was, whom could she call? She walked to the door.

'Will you open the door, please?'

She saw the handle turn, and knew that he would be angry that she had locked it.

91

'What do you want?'

'To come in,' said Stranragh. 'I won't – I'm not angry with you.'

She turned the key with both hands. For a second they both looked at each other as if some unexpected change might have occurred to either, or both of them, over the last few days. Georgiana stood back to let him pass her, and then walked slowly over to her bed and sat down.

She was frightened at the way he was looking at her, as if he had made up his mind and his resolution had brought about some objectivity as far as he was concerned, some detachment that had removed him from her.

'I've brought you some flowers. Freesias.'

He said the name of the flower as if she might, since her illness, have forgotten what they were called. He put a small basket of them beside her bed. He must have driven miles to get them, she thought. Not at all like James, who disliked anyone taking a car anywhere unless it was for some immensely practical reason. Freesias were not practical. But, she thought, they could be meant to soothe or to lull her into a sense of his having only her happiness at heart. She guessed that he was about to explain that the reason he had behaved as he had was pure frustration, and that she had made him very unhappy. Extremely unhappy. He would pause after that so that Georgiana could take in the awfulness of making someone like James unhappy. And then he would recommend something, she thought, something that would be very much for 'her own good'.

He sat down on the chair that Dr McCulloch normally occupied. Georgiana found herself resenting this, as if he had taken a seat that she had been 'keeping' for someone else. James, with his dreadful cross of Etonian pomposity and Scottish dourness, would never tell her stories such as the good doctor told her – old folk tales of shoes that were stolen by small people, of women who hid their shawls (women who had come from the sea), of lights left on in windows for lovers that never returned. That was not a Scotland that James could talk about. To him, and landowners like him, being 'Scottish' was attending the Highland Ball in his grandfather's kilt.

'We have not opened our account in a very auspicious way.'

James cleared his throat. He liked to talk to Georgiana as if she were a board meeting. When they first met she had found it almost endearing, because she knew that it was because he had been an only child, and had heard grown-ups speak to each other like that and decided to copy it.

'I don't know what you mean.'

'Our joint account, our married life, has not begun very—'

'It hasn't begun at all.'

James sighed. He hated to be interrupted.

'We should close down this account, and start again.'

'Oh, I don't think so,' said Georgiana in the vague way that girls do when they have decided that they don't think their shoes go with their coat, or their blouse with their jacket.

'I am in disagreement with you.'

Georgiana smiled, and looked at him.

'It's not your fault, James, it's my fault, and there's very little more to be said about it.'

He looked at her, surprised. For the first time he sensed in her a quality he had not expected.

'What do you mean by that?'

'Only that these last disastrous months are my fault. You can divorce me. I won't ask anything of you. After all, as you said so often – it must be my fault. A man cannot be blamed.'

'I don't want a divorce.'

'You must do. Anyone—' She was about to say 'normal', when she stopped.

'My step-mother is calling tomorrow, and she wishes to see you.'

Georgiana lay back against the pillows. She was twenty-three, she had had two lovers and a marriage, and yet it had only just occurred to her that James might be abnormal, in a medical sense. She had never read a medical book, and had always considered that psychiatry was something silly that Americans went in for. She would have to ask Dr McCulloch about it tomorrow, she thought excitedly, because if James was abnormal, then it meant that she wasn't, might not be, as repulsive as she thought.

'I don't want to see your step-mother.'

'Why not, may I ask? She has been very concerned about you.'

'Dr McCulloch says I am to have no visitors.'

'Dr McCulloch is a country doctor who knows as much about medicine as I do.'

Georgiana was silent. The memory of that night a few weeks ago was coming back to her. It was coming back to her again, and the small stand that she was making against James was making her feel weak. She felt faint and ill, and she couldn't see parts of the room, or she thought she couldn't, which was just as bad.

'Whatever you wish,' she said, hoping this would send him away.

'Good. Now no more talk of closing our account together, please.'

He turned by the door.

'And I would recommend you change your nightdress before her visit. The lace on the left shoulder is torn. It needs to be mended. If you could give it to Mrs Peebles, please.'

He closed the door behind him, and Georgiana closed her eyes. A visit from the man with the scythe would be more welcome than her step-mother-in-law.

But witches do swim across the Styx, and Georgiana knew this the next day when she heard Mrs Peebles, her voice kept at a low Celtic murmur, escorting the Dowager up the stairs and along the corridor to her room. Mrs Peebles did not like Georgiana, any more than did the Dowager Lady Stranragh, and so they entered the room in complete accord, their manner suggesting that they were both members of the same secret society. Girls like Georgiana were not to their taste. They suspected them, they sensed that they were bored by the important things in life, like bookkeeping and bottling, and mending and patching; and that men liked them.

'She has never once asked to see the household accounts,' Mrs Peebles complained frequently to the girls who came to help. 'And yet she has forbidden all re-use of fats, and the left-overs have to be fed to the dog.'

Georgiana had changed her nightdress, and as she lay

against her lace pillows the Dowager was sorry to see that she looked very beautiful. What a bad day it was on which James had met her. And how wonderful it would be if she had something very bad wrong with her, she thought, something that would lead to her early death and replacement by someone of the Dowager's choice.

'Good morning, Georgiana.'

Georgiana looked at her. Try as she might she couldn't help being frightened by the Dowager. The fact that most people were was no comfort. She was glad she was in bed, and that she could clench her hands under the bedclothes without her being able to see.

'Good morning.'

'Not yet well, I hear,' the Dowager purred, sitting her tall frame down on a corner chair as if she wanted to take a long, detached view of Georgiana's condition.

'Not quite, no.'

'You've been in bed a great deal, a great deal. I wonder what it can be?'

'Cancer probably,' said Georgiana flippantly. 'Unhappy people get cancer, don't they? That's what you usually say.'

'Oh, I don't think so,' said the Dowager hopefully. 'Have you lost weight?'

'Masses.'

'Ah, well then, perhaps there is cause for worry.'

She looked at Mrs Peebles and smiled.

'Just as well Lord Stranragh has booked her ladyship into that clinic in Edinburgh, isn't it?'

'Yes, just as well,' said Mrs Peebles, 'just as well.'

'Has he told Dr McCulloch?' Georgiana's face registered mild interest.

'No, but he intends to when he calls this afternoon. And not a moment too soon, in my opinion.'

Georgiana looked out of the window. It was beginning to rain again, as it always seemed to. If only Dr McCulloch would come to see her before he saw James.

'Well now, I expect we've tired you.'

Georgiana said nothing, and the two women left her bedroom, their departure leaving behind a sense of panic and fear that not even their arrival had engendered. Georgiana knew about clinics. Friends, sisters of friends, people she had heard about, were put into clinics, private clinics, and sane people were certified insane, and well people became ill, and they gave you injections and electric shocks, and you spent the rest of your life as a half-person This was Stranragh's way of revenging himself. His pride could not allow for a divorce due to his inability to have what Dr McCulloch referred to, in biblical terms, as 'conjugation', but it would not be hurt by a certificate that pronounced her insane.

The time of Dr McCulloch's visit came and was, it seemed to her, about to go, before the door opened and his tall raincoated figure stood enshrined in the doorway. He closed the door after him, as he always did, and then he took a chair and brought it to her bedside, as he always did. They had their usual conversation, and then he took out his thermometer, and as he did so he leant forward and whispered.

'He's outside the door.'

Georgiana knew then that she had no hope. If James was outside the door then he had already seen Dr McCulloch, and he would have informed (one of James's favourite words) Dr McCulloch of his intention to have Georgiana moved to a clinic. Now no-one could save her. In books the heroines always had someone waiting for them, or someone they could telephone for rescue and, after managing a few words, quickly replace the receiver. But life, as she had discovered since she married James, was not at all like books, probably because if it were no-one would bother to read them.

She stared at Dr McCulloch over the top of the thermometer. He had stopped whispering, and was now settling down as if to continue telling her one of his stories of Scottish life.

'I have told Lord Stranragh,' he said, fixing her sternly with his pale blue eyes, 'that the greatest care must be taken of you in your condition. Obviously you have not had the most felicitous start to your pregnancy, what with the "fall" and everything, but I can see no reason why you should not, after proper bed rest, continue to full term and deliver yourself of a bonny baby of good weight.'

He removed the thermometer from Georgiana's mouth.

'I have also told him that my reason for not informing him of the intended event was I was not altogether sure, after the fall, that you would not miscarry. However, now that you are gaining weight a little and beginning to sit up and take notice, and with the summer coming on, I would say that all should be well.'

He leant forward again, and as he put the thermometer away he whispered, 'Don't let me down now, or all is lost.'

Georgiana attempted a smile.

'And was Lord Stranragh pleased, Doctor McCulloch?'

'Naturally, Lady Stranragh. He went to tell the Dowager the good news straightaway.'

'I am afraid I was very naughty and teased her this morning that I had something seriously wrong.'

Dr McCulloch nodded, and then continued.

'I have recommended to his lordship that you need to get away. To get some sun. It will help build you up for the pregnancy.'

'And what was his answer?'

'He has agreed to take you to his house in Italy for a few weeks' sunshine. And once there—'

The doctor leant forward once again and seemed to be examining the exact amount of iron tablets left in Georgiana's medicine bottle.

'And once there,' he whispered, 'you can run away.'

# 5

The calendar of events for the village of Flint was sometimes too sensational in nature even for the Vicar, who, although he prided himself upon being the stone that created the ripples in their little community (an analogy which he much favoured in his sermons) nevertheless, upon occasion, he sometimes found himself regretting that so many of his parishioners had such fertile imaginations when it came to fund raising.

Long before the Charity Barbecue held by the Ancient Monument and sponsored by Wiltshire Whoppers, there had been the Shrove Tuesday Pancake Race, which had left so many crêpes by the roadside that, as Elliott remarked, 'it looked as if a rather funny herd of cows had passed by'.

Then there had been the Lenten Fast, or Freeze In as it was known in the Queen's Arms. This entailed the Vicar and his wife sitting in the church in silent fast, warmed by only one bar of the electric fire kindly lent for the occasion by Margaret Paine, who, although anxious to identify with world suffering, nevertheless found herself unable to join them. A cold prevented her from leaving her television set, and a bad attack of gout in her elbow confined Jane Dupont to *her* armchair, where she nevertheless managed to change channels on her remote control with her usual dexterity.

Fulton and Elliott had joined the Vicar and his wife for a controlled experiment in fasting, but had taken the precaution of bringing along their own three-bar fire and a thermos filled with a special sort of coffee, which they kept hidden by a hassock. They had decided to support the Vicar in his fast, not just because they too disapproved of world suffering, but because they wanted their christening to go without a hitch.

'You never know with vicars,' Fulton had warned Elliott while they were climbing into their maximum weight thermal underwear. 'They have only to be presented with a christening, or a wedding, to suddenly decide to ban the event on the grounds that Jesus doesn't want us for a moonbeam, or something. And I don't want Victoria to have anything but the best start.'

'Of course we don't,' said Elliott approvingly.

Now she was safely delivered, Victoria Eugenia Lucia (this last name was on Elliott's insistence) was the light of their lives and the centre of their existence, and the christening would have to be a major event in the village with everyone invited; at least to the church.

Lady Tizzy's homecoming had been more than just the usual re-entrance of a happy mother firmly safety-pinned back into a pair of old jeans with front buttoning smock to cover. The day before her return the whole house had been spring cleaned, as if Elliott was determined to eliminate any germs that might be found to be hiding beyond the reach of sponge mop or feather duster. Then the wooden floors had been polished on hands and knees by everyone except the monthly nurse, who had been sacked after only one day for refusing to admit that her fingernails were a health hazard. No new nurse had been engaged, but Nanny had been gracious enough to arrive three weeks early, with her own kettle and hairdryer, and commendably short fingernails.

The bluebird of happiness sat once more upon the old tiled roof of Flint House as Patti and Victoria, sitting safely in the back of the newly purchased old Bentley, were driven proudly up the short carriage drive to be received by Nanny and Elliott, who was in such a state of excitement that he (and Nanny) had been forced to have a 'little something' even before the great arrival.

Victoria was handed over to Nanny and Patti was handed over to Elliott, then both were whisked upstairs for a rest, while downstairs Fulton inspected all the arrangements, as if he fully expected the baby to put in for adoption should she find the flower arrangements not to her liking.

A bottle of champagne was produced from the drinks fridge, then both men mounted the stairs to the nursery to 'watch Nanny'.

'I'm not sure about those new bottles with the bags,' said Fulton afterwards, as if he had a vast experience with some other range.

'No, nor am I,' said Elliott. 'But Nanny likes them to start with, and then she likes to go back to the others later.'

'And I'm not sure about those new French nappies.'

'No, nor am I,' agreed Elliott. 'But Nanny – well, we'll just have to let her give them a try.'

'I don't know why but I'm always suspicious of anything foreign in the nursery.'

'I'm a *little* disappointed in the Duc de Berry cradle, if you really want to know.'

'Oh, no, why?'

'I don't know. It doesn't look so good, now it's got a baby in it.'

'I don't think cradles ever do.'

'Perhaps not.'

'Well. Now we've had the homecoming, we'll have to start planning the christening.'

'Godparents. We haven't even thought of them.'

'The Countess, naturally.'

'Of course.'

'The Marchioness?'

'No, that would be a clash.'

'How about his lordship?'

'Why not?'

'Why not indeed.'

'So.'

Fulton quickly took a pad on his knee and started to write in his best 'menu' writing.

'The infant daughter of Mr and Mrs Fulton Montrose-Benedict-Cavanagh—'

'I don't know where you got all your names from, but they do look good written,' said Elliott.

'From the telephone book, like everyone else.'

'I've just kept to Stanhope like the Gate, because everyone's heard of it.'

'So, we've got one Countess, one Marquis, and now we need someone like a Major or a Colonel, or it'll look too Debrett for words.'

Fulton held up his list in front of him and stared at it critically.

'I suppose we'll have to ask Lady Tizzy whether or not she wants to choose someone,' said Elliott doubtfully.

'Must we?'

'Oh, I think we must.'

'I'm not sure if that's your *best* idea to date.'

'Just one, just one little one.'

'Oh very well, but don't blame me if it throws the entire proceedings into social jeopardy.'

'Nothing unusual in that. Social jeopardy's Patti's middle name.'

Which was how the notice in *The Times* eventually came to read:

> The infant daughter of Mr and Mrs Fulton Montrose-Benedict-Cavanagh was christened Victoria Eugenia Lucia. Godparents in attendance were the Countess of Cosborough, the Marquis of Pemberton, Major Newnes-William, and Mr Bert Dean.

'Who is Bert Dean?' Elliott asked Patti when she submitted her choice.

'He's the porter at the flat where Knightey and I used to live before we moved down here.'

'How charming.'

'Well, he's never been to the country, so I thought it would be nice.'

Patti finished painting her last toenail and looked up at Elliott. She had hidden her tapestry under the bed, well out of sight of Elliott's prying eyes. Whatever happened she did not want Elliott finding out about it and taking it over the way he took over everything. A few months ago she'd tried making the baby some bootees, but she hadn't even got to the cornering before he undid it all and then re-did it all, and then finished it. Much as she loved Elliott, and she did, nothing was your own when he was around.

'I'm going to the nursery to see the baby. Coming?'

Patti waved her feet in various directions to dry them, and then nodded. She'd already seen the baby *once* today, but if it made Elliott happy, then she would go to the nursery again, with him.

'What are you wearing for the christening?' she asked him on the way.

'Oh, we thought we'd all wear our wedding suits.'

'I'm not wearing mine, it'll be too big now.'

'That's the trouble with getting married when you're pregnant, nothing fits afterwards.'

'I was hoping Fulton would buy me a new dress, and a hat. You know, the kind that Royals wear when they go to visit schools and hospitals.'

Elliott put his arm round her and kissed her lightly.

'You have what you want,' he said warmly, and then just as they reached the nursery door he smiled. 'Oh, by the way, John Pemberton's said yes to being a godfather. That's nice, isn't it?'

'I suppose so,' said Patti.

'You didn't want Andrew Gillott, did you?'

'No. No, no-one in their right mind would want him.'

'That's just what I thought,' said Elliott. 'Morning, Nanny.'

Nanny smiled. She loved working for gentlemen, they were so much easier than women. A nice widower was the tops, of course, but if you couldn't find one of those, and they did seem to be rare, then there was no doubt two nice 'boys' like Mr Fulton and Mr Elliott were the very next best thing.

'I've bought you something I thought you'd appreciate.'

Elliott handed Nanny a small, perfectly wrapped parcel which Nanny opened excitedly. Inside was a beautiful little silk dress and bonnet.

'I knew you'd like it,' Elliott smiled. 'I did all the drawn thread work round the edge myself.'

Nanny held up the dress.

'It's quite, quite beautiful, and she'll look a picture in it. Won't she, Lady Tisbury?'

Patti nodded and yawned. Personally she found all the fuss over baby-clothes a bit silly. After all, when all was said and done the baby only grew out of the things, and when it wasn't growing out of things, it was doing other things, things that quite took your mind off what it was wearing. Still, if it made Fulton and Elliott and Nanny happy, then that was all right. She yawned again, and her mind turned to Ron, the policeman who'd taken her to hospital. He'd been to see her in the Clinic before she left. He was tall, and handsome, and young. Something she'd never gone for before. Trouble was how would she tell the 'boys'?

Jennifer looked across the lawn at Pember. He was being terribly irritating, as usual. Sitting quietly under a tree reading his book, and not saying anything to anyone. She chose a new wool for her tapestry. Bright pink, and even brighter in the sunlight. Life had been intensely dull of late since Georgiana had returned to Scotland. Of course she had had the usual 'bread and butter' letter from her, but no real news. A brief mention of Stranragh killing things, but nothing about the state of the marriage, or whether she had taken Jennifer's advice, or not taken Jennifer's advice. It was most frustrating, and not even the christening of Lady Tizzy's baby or the Countess moving to neighbouring Dorset, not even these normally riveting events could keep her mentally amused.

Of course it was terribly like Georgiana, and if she hadn't known her all her life she might have felt hurt instead of just frustrated, but as it was she realized it was only to be expected from one who, it had to be faced, was and always would be more than a little selfish. The comparison with Lady Caroline Lamb came to mind as it had many times before. She too, it appeared, had had a way of using people emotionally and then moving on and leaving them. No doubt (Jennifer sucked hard on the end of the pink wool which was refusing to push its way into the top of her needle), no doubt if poor Pember had not met her (Jennifer that is), he would have ended up like that poor Melbourne, worn to a threadpaper and having a city in Australia named after him, instead of being as he was, which although irritating to her personally, was not when all was said and done as bad as Melbourne had been by all accounts, it seemed.

'Pember?'

Pemberton failed to look up at his wife. As with most women, she could not bear to see him happy. He had only to be seen with a book or a newspaper, particularly a newspaper, or a nice crisp copy of *Horse and Hound* or *Pacemaker*, and before long he knew he would be hearing her less than dulcet tones. He had started to affect a slight deafness, but it had not had the desired effect of putting her off, rather it had encouraged her, and she, as she was doing now, merely raised her voice to a piercing level, a level that reminded him most vividly of her mother.

'Pember?'

'No.'

Jennifer pierced the pink flower on the canvas. Pember might be an aristocrat, and he might like to go on and on about having Plantagenet blood, but as far as she was concerned he was rude. And if that's what having Plantagenet blood made you, then you were better off without it.

'Pember, wouldn't it be nice if we walked round the garden together and talked and things?'

'No.'

Jennifer made a half cross-stitch. If he was in that kind of mood then there was nothing more to say. There would have been a time, not so long ago, when she would have been really hurt by his attitude, but nowadays this was not so. She had learnt to grow a tougher hide. She had had to, for being a Marchioness was not all beer and skittles, or rather champagne and croquet; although reading about the so-called 'privileged' in the newspapers, anyone would think it was. Just as if being rich prevented you from being human too. Just as if private doctors and dentists, and not having to do your own washing-up, solved every problem. Yes, it was true, you could afford to charter a private plane and go anywhere in the world you wanted, but what everyone forgot to remember was that you *still had to come back*. It wasn't as if when you got back all your problems had vanished. There were still the same responsibilities, still the same worries. Was Bloss a secret drinker? Was Irene in the village shop taking advantage of their custom and overcharging? Had the portraits in the Long Gallery been badly varnished? Was Pember right about the Water Garden having been made to look like something in a London park? Should she have her mother to stay while Andrew was helping the Countess move in? It was problems of this kind that no aeroplane, however privately chartered, could fly you away from. *So* different from how people, other people who lived in simpler conditions, imagined.

'Are you sure you don't want to have a little walk round the garden with me?'

'Quite sure, thank you.'

'Very well.'

Pember looked up. He always looked up when Jennifer said very well like that. It was a nasty clipped sort of very well, and then she closed her lips together. 'Got a mouth like a rat trap', his mother used to say of her. His mother hadn't liked her.

'What do you mean, very well?'

Jennifer gave a mocking little laugh.

'Just that, Pember.'

'No, not just that. You said very well, and very well does not mean just that.'

'Very well means very well in plain English, Pember. And if you don't know that, everyone else does.'

'Yes, I know that, but what I mean is – it's the way you said it. It meant something else, the way you said it. What did it mean?'

Jennifer gave another little laugh, less mocking, but more amused.

'If,' she said triumphantly, 'you had come round the

garden with me, no doubt you would have found out. But since you didn't, you haven't. Ah good, here's Bloss with the post.'

Bloss presented her with the letters. She had tried to make him present them to her on a salver, like in the old days, like in West End plays and serials on television, but Bloss was a stickler on this point and he would not co-operate, any more than she could get him to agree with the way she liked the table set, or where her guests should sit.

'There are no such things as old servants, only old masters,' the Countess had said the other day, just as Jennifer had finished complaining about Bloss. And that had seemed to put an end to the matter for all of them, except Bloss. Perhaps if she had been there before Bloss, things might have been different, but such, alas, had not been the case. In fact very far from it, so far from it that when she was a young bride, on certain occasions Jennifer had had the distinct impression that Bloss had hired her, and that if she did not respond to the way he saw things, he would have no hesitation in firing her.

Jennifer rifled through the letters, knowing Pember was watching her, and knowing at the same time that he was too proud to ask her for them.

'All boring,' she said, throwing them on a chair.

Pember strolled nonchalantly across to the chair, before snatching them up.

'Not so,' he said. It was quite extraordinary to be able to take that attitude, and quite frankly, only a woman could.

'Very boring,' said Jennifer firmly, 'except for this.'

She waggled a highly coloured postcard at him.

'Italy,' she said. 'Georgiana is in Italy.'

Pember waved the letters back at her from under his tree.

'Business,' he said. 'Money, shares; keeps Jennifer.'

But his light sarcasm was lost on Jennifer who was now engrossed in trying to translate Georgiana's large sloping handwriting, so reminiscent of barbed-wire entanglements.

She had not been very well, the postcard said. 'Dear James' had brought her out to his house in Tuscany to help her get better, because, 'guess what?' (Jennifer couldn't), she was pregnant. This word was followed by a host of Georgiana's usual exclamation marks.

'Good heavens,' said Jennifer slowly, knowing that Pember would be forced to look up. 'Georgiana's pregnant.'

Even Pemberton now had to give her his attention.

'But I thought the whole point was that he *couldn't*.'

'Please, Pember—' Jennifer waved the postcard around her face in the manner of a fan. 'Please.'

'Well, that's what you two girls were always going on about, wasn't it?'

'No, we were not.'

'But—'

Pemberton was just about to say, 'But Bloss said so', when he remembered that he wasn't meant to know, so he stopped.

'We didn't "go on", as you put it, about anything. That wasn't what we were going on about at all.'

'Oh. What was it then?'

'Nothing.'

'Oh.'

'We were merely discussing some of Georgiana's problems.'

'If you ask me, Georgiana's only ever had one problem – no money.'

'Please, Pember, don't be vulgar.'

'It's true,' Pemberton persisted.

'Maybe, but now she's got two.'

She looked across at Pember.

'You knew she was pregnant of course?'

Pemberton groaned. He hated pregnant women.

'No,' he said. 'But how ghastly.'

'What *do* you mean?'

'Just that. Ghastly.'

'I heard you, Pember, I heard you the first time.'

'Then why did you say, "what d'you mean"?'

'Probably because,' said Jennifer slowly, 'I couldn't believe what I heard.'

'All right, all right, but pregnancy is women's palaver, and let's face it, she doesn't like the chap, or he doesn't like her, whichever or whatever, and there's no sense in thinking that it's a good idea to have a baby when you don't like each other.'

'Oh—'

'Now what?'

'Bilge.'

'Bilge?'

'Yes, bilge.'

'Are you feeling all right?'

'No I'm not.'

'No, I thought you weren't.'

'No I'm not.'

'I thought you couldn't be.'

'Oh *did* you?'

'Yes, I did. It's not like you to say – what's it—'

'Bilge?'

'Yes, that's right, you don't normally—'

'If it's any of your business, which I sometimes wonder, I am not feeling all right, because *I* am pregnant.'

Pemberton put his head in his hands and groaned.

'Not again.'

Jennifer stood up and walked across to him, and much against her principles, for she was wearing new shoes, she kicked Pemberton sharply on the ankle. Unfortunately for his lordship, the newly purchased footwear was in the style that favours a point at the front. Jennifer had not been noted for her excellence at games at Grantley Abbey, but unhappily for Pemberton, even she was unable to miss his nearest ankle.

Bloss was about to open the french windows on to the lawn, bringing with him his lordship's usual lunch-time bevvy, when he became an amazed witness to her ladyship's assault. He turned quickly to stop himself laughing, and then with an admirable sense of what is fitting, he turned back to the drinks table and topped up Pemberton's drink, because there was no doubt that he would be needing it, and even more than usual.

'Do I look Royal?' asked Patti.

She turned her head for Elliott to see her new hat. Elliott sighed inwardly. Patti could make a tiara look sheer Woolworths. She was beautiful, of course, but she had no class as in breeding.

'No, you don't look Royal,' said Elliott. 'But if you tilt the hat you could look stunning.'

Patti smiled at her image in the mirror. The previous evening, while the boys were learning how to bath the baby, she had telephoned Ron and he had agreed to meet. But first they had the excitement of the christening.

'Victoria Eugenia?' said the Countess. 'Whatever next? I thought it would be something a little less flamboyant, less Empress-in-exile, less *grande dame* and more "wild flower", considering the mother was a Bluebell girl.'

'I hate flower names,' said Fulton, determined not to be put down on their big day. 'Although Potentilla might be nice.'

'If you didn't know what it was, Diarrhoea would be very pretty,' said Elliott.

'I think we've had quite enough of that,' said the Countess, sensing defeat. 'Where's the Vicar?'

'We're meeting him at St Balsam's.'

'Yes, of course,' murmured the Countess, 'no family chapel.'

The cars came to the door, and Patti and Fulton shared theirs with Nanny and the baby, while Elliott followed with the Countess.

'I forgot to ask you who else has the honour to be a godparent?' The Countess powdered her nose over-liberally, leaving little pieces of powder puff on the end of her nose, but she was not in the sort of mood where Elliott could tell her.

'Oh just John Pemberton, yourself, and Major Bill, and Bert.'

'Oh good, Bert, I didn't know *he* was coming.'

Elliott hooted suddenly, and conscientiously, as they came to a blind corner. He knew that the Countess could not possibly know Bert Dean, the head porter at Patti's old flat. He also knew that her Bert was a really rather different Bert, a dear old friend who wouldn't have had much experience in lift work, or polishing hand rails, or any of the other duties at which, doubtless, Patti's Bert was more than adept. She was in such a difficult mood he couldn't bring himself to tell her that it wasn't her Bert, so he quickly changed the subject instead.

'Oh by the way, the father is not Andrew Gillott.'

'I know *that*,' said the Countess. 'Everyone knows that.'

'Yes, but no-one knows who it really is,' said Elliott.

'It's not Fulton's, is it?'

Elliott smiled. 'It looks so like him at the moment, I'm seriously beginning to wonder. They had a raging affair when I was in Florence.'

'You can't have an affair if you're married,' was all the Countess would say, and as they were now at the village church and the Vicar was standing outside smiling, there was very little time for anything else.

'I hate vicars,' said the Countess. 'I always think they do it to get out of the Army. Good afternoon, good afternoon.' She nodded briskly at the prelate.

'Lovely afternoon for it, isn't it?' said the Vicar.

'Yes,' said the Countess, 'but you don't really need it for a christening, bit of a waste, really.'

'Nevertheless, look up, God is smiling on us, m'lady.'

The Vicar gave an involuntary little bow. Just very small, to acknowledge the Countess's precedence.

'I'm just going to take a little walk round the

115

graveyard. One or two people I know here.' The Countess placed her hand on Elliott's arm. 'Glad to see you haven't planted it out with pelargoniums, and made it look like a pub.'

They walked off towards the graveyard.

'I didn't know he was Welsh,' said the Countess. 'You want to watch that. He'll start baptising the child with weird names, and singing rugby songs.'

'He's not,' said Elliott.

'He said "look you".'

'No he didn't. He said "look up". He always says that. Something to do with the Renaissance and not looking at the ground all the time. You know.'

'Sounds an ass, like all vicars,' grumbled the Countess.

'He's quite sweet, really.'

The Countess stopped in front of a tombstone.

'Ah yes, here's old Roley,' she said. She peered at the inscription. 'How old was he? I haven't got my *lunettes*.'

Elliott did a small piece of mental arithmetic.

'Eighty-three.'

He was just about to say a good age when he remembered the Countess was in the latish seventies, so he stopped. She sighed.

'Poor old chap, quite young really.'

'Yes, quite young,' Elliott agreed, adding a second later, 'considering.'

The Countess looked at him sharply.

'Considering what?'

'You know, considering that he could have been – older.'

'His father lived till he was a hundred and two, and he'd still be alive today if he hadn't overdone it at the centenary party.'

'Must have been quite a party.'

The Countess smiled.

'Yes, we all had a good time. Of course, it was properly done. He booked the caterers for a week, and the only people who got tired were the young; but that didn't matter because they just slept it off in the hay barns until they were ready to start again. Nice chap, old Roley's father, but a devil with the maids. Poor old Maude tried everything, but it didn't make any difference. Ugly, old, deaf or cross, the moment they put on their uniforms it was la, la, boompsy daisy.'

She walked on and Elliott followed her, peering as he always did, almost superstitiously, at the ages of the lately departed and the not so lately departed.

'The Wiltshire air seems to be very good for people. They all live to a good age,' he remarked cheerfully.

Fulton waved at them from the church gate.

'Time to do your bit,' he called to the Countess.

'One thing I never thought I'd be is godmother to one of Fulton's children.'

'No,' Elliott agreed. 'It does seem a bit of a fairy story, doesn't it?'

The parish church of Flint was Norman in origin. It was plain and it was sturdy, an unaffected host to the christening of Victoria Eugenia Lucia Montrose-Benedict-Cavanagh. Her christening robe, in contrast to the church and the font, was long, elaborate and Victorian. It had been in Pemberton's family since the late eighteen-eighties, and Jennifer had kindly loaned it for

117

the occasion, a gesture that had been appreciated by everyone concerned, with the exception of Lady Tizzy, who maintained that it was too good for a baby.

In spite of her reservations about the Vicar, the Countess found herself enjoying the service. Perhaps the fact that she had been invited to be a godmother secretly pleased her more than she would admit, for at her age it was not something that occurred very often, any more than being given diamonds, or acquiring a new boy-friend; or perhaps it was the church itself.

Its simplicity pleased her. Its air of having given (one faded regimental standard at the back) to the common cause of England, while not giving itself airs or graces. The hassocks had been stitched over the past century by the seemingly endless supply of good ladies that parishes such as Flint were always, somehow, able to recruit; its windows kindly donated by families anxious to record their part in the life of the parish, and its organ by an American gentleman from Ohio who, it seemed, was a distant relation of the original Flints and had consequently been allowed to be buried in the churchyard. History had left its mark on some of the tombs: knights who had been mistaken for saints, and had their carved stone noses and fingers knocked off for their pains, ladies in wimples with toes missing. High above them and out of reach of the zealot's eager swipe, shone the stained glass saints of yesterday. But even they were not untouched, for no-one had seen fit to replace their saintly coloured glass with anything but the plainest kind, so that halos half-shone and hands held in benediction were largely left to the onlooker's imagination. And, over all, the kindly English light softened the sad brass plaques that told of sons' lives given proudly for their fathers' causes. Flowers and water, 'who giveth this child in baptism', starched white linen clothes, deep proud lace upon the baby's hand-stitched robes. Heritage, recognizable, unfussed, and unproud.

'I christen thee Victoria Eugenia—' a small pause, 'Lucia.'

Elliott smiled as the Vicar said 'Lucia', as if to say 'ha, ha,' to Fulton; but no-one noticed, for the baby was yelling, and Nanny was quite sure that she should have brought a bottle of boiled water, as she had originally intended.

'Home for lots of nice things,' said Fulton to everyone and no-one, after they had all posed for the photographs outside the church.

'I couldn't see Bert at all,' said the Countess, getting back into Elliott's car.

'Oh, couldn't you?' said Elliott innocently.

'It's probably because I've brought my wrong glasses.'

'Unfortunately he can't stay for tea,' said Elliott without even having to cross his fingers. 'He's got to get back.'

'Beastly wife of his, she's stark staring mad as a hatter. I'm surprised she let him come at all. She's got some bee in her bonnet that he's always having affairs.'

'Really?'

'He should have had her put away years ago.'

'Is he always having affairs?'

'Of course.'

There was a small pause as the Countess tried to do up her seat belt and failed, so that Elliott had to do it

119

for her, all the while pretending that it was *his* fault that she couldn't do it up.

'Well then—'

Elliott drove slowly forward following the long line of cars.

'Now we know.'

'Do we?'

'Of course. You must have noticed. I know I did. I mean no-one could fail to, really. I mean it isn't just the nose, it's *everything*. I mean even her hands, the long fingers, *everything*.'

Elliott could suddenly feel that he was about to get terribly excited, in the way that he sometime's did when the telephone rang and he knew it was going to be good news.

'I was so busy praying, I can't say I noticed anything.'

'Of course, from Fulton's point of view it will be a great relief, because it has to be faced, with Lady Tizzy being what she is, it could have been the milkman. But as it is, with blood like that coursing through her veins, he has not got much to fear. And at least you *know*. I mean – what a comfort!'

Elliott couldn't wait to be comforted, even though he had not until now known that he was in need of it. His eyes left the road and the car plunged towards the hedgerows at the side.

'You don't mean Victoria is a—'

'Oh, but I do. And after all, I should know, I knew his father, and his grandfather, and most of his uncles.'

'Gracious heavens.'

Elliott steered the car away from the looming tangle of briars and bush. If the Countess was right, it was incredibly exciting, for you-know-who, to whom she was referring, had Plantagenet blood absolutely coursing through his veins in great blue rivulets, which meant that at least half of Victoria's rivulets were also bright, bright blue. He couldn't wait to tell Fulton.

'Well?'

'Well.'

The christening tea had been a huge success, nothing to do with the tea, but everything to do with the vintage champagne that Fulton had insisted upon serving. Nanny had held the baby throughout, and Patti had sat next to her wearing not only her new hat, but an appropriately gracious smile to go with it. She loved the baby, just so long as Nanny was left holding it. The guests had mingled and mixed really very well, considering they nearly all not only knew each other, but saw each other most of the time. They adopted surprised tones at everything, which helped to conceal both this fact and also the fact that they were, by nature, to a person, not in the habit of being surprised by anything.

Now Fulton stood by the chimneypiece, a fresh glass of champagne à la main, and waited with well-concealed impatience to hear Elliott's news. It had to be good, because Elliott was staring at his fingernails and admiring his half-moons, which he only did on special occasions.

'She's a—'

'Who is?'

'Your – our daughter. Victoria Eugenia *Lucia* is a Melbury. She's Pemberton's by-blow.'

'Oh yes, and I'm the King of Mesopotamia.'

'The Countess is never wrong.'

Fulton looked at Elliott. He knew, as Elliott knew, that the Countess had spread the rumour that Gillott was Victoria's father only to them, and simply and solely to annoy them, in which she had succeeded admirably. On the other hand, he also knew that now they had made the Countess the fairy godmother, she would not continue to annoy them but would, in her inimitable way, give them her sole support, even to the point when they would no doubt wish, quite heartily, that she wouldn't. She would bring Shetland shawls and christening spoons, and frocks hand-smocked with threads of silk. She would collect a pearl for her every birthday, and a share certificate every Christmas, but would she also send her Plantagenet blood? Was she the kind of countess that could not have borne to be a fairy godmother to any but the most thoroughbred? He wanted to believe that it was all true, and yet he couldn't let himself, because if it was true, then it was really too good to be true.

'But when could they have – I mean, *when*?'

'That's exactly what I was wondering. And then, just now, I said to myself how ridiculous, they could have met anywhere, frequently, they only live five miles apart.'

'Mind you, while we were at the font,' said Fulton excitedly, 'while we were there, and Pemberton was looking down at the baby, he did look frightfully soppy, but I thought it was because christenings can get people like that. You know.'

'You see, I think he accepted to be the godfather to put Jennifer off the scent.'

'Clever.'

'That's what I thought.'

'Oh, I don't know, we mustn't get too excited. After all, the old tabby might be wrong. You know, she's not always right about everything, although you'd never guess it from what she says.'

'But the fingers, the nails, those long Melbury fingers.'

'Shall we go and find Patti, and talk around and about it?'

'No, that would be fatal. No, we'll just have to wait and see, and if we're right, it'll soon become pretty obvious.'

'Where is Lady Tizzy, anyway?'

'Oh, I don't know. She said something about having to slip out for a breath of fresh air.'

Fulton went to the window and stared out into the garden. Life had been pretty kind to him lately. It had sent him a new direction at an age when most men were wondering if anything nice was ever going to happen to them again. He had a wife, a best friend, and now a daughter who might be so aristocratic (albeit *bar sinistra*) that her forebears went back well over a thousand years. He hardly dared believe his good fortune, and because he couldn't, he quickly tried to think of any bad things that could happen, to prevent them happening. And then he saw a magpie sitting on a branch just above the herbaceous border, so he quickly made a little spitting noise, to undo the bad luck of not seeing a pair.

# 6

In Italy, while Georgiana planned her escape from him, Stranragh became her tutor. It could not be helped, for they began her convalescence in Florence, and Georgiana knew nothing about Florence except that it reminded her of Bath. She was bored, of course, but had to pretend not to be. She did not have any fondness for architecture, once it was removed from the purely domestic, and so it was not surprising that Stranragh was unable to ignite her interest; for if she couldn't convert the Baptistry (perhaps adding much-needed festoon blinds), or paint the Loggia del Bigallo a very, very, pale pink wash, they succeeded only in making her feel dutifully admiring.

Stranragh failed to notice her lack of interest but, positioning her beneath the marble lantern of the cupola of the Cathedral for example, he would happily lecture her on Brunelleschi's dramas over its construction before walking her off to some new revelation. Of course she realised that he was doing this because she was no longer just his, but the future (in his mind) mother of his son (for of course she would have to have a son).

Georgiana tried not to despise Stranragh for his sudden rather nauseating concern for her, and failed. Nevertheless it was difficult to become preoccupied with such emotions when there was sunshine. After Scotland it was almost unbelievable to be in a place where she no longer had to wear layer upon layer of clothing, but could make even the business of whether or not to take a cardigan to put over her shoulders a decision of a momentous nature.

'Do you think I should?'

'Yes, I think you should.'

'But won't it be a nuisance?'

'Perhaps, but on the other hand if you don't take it you might feel cold suddenly.'

'Oh, very well, perhaps you're right.'

'No, stay there,' James paused, 'I'll fetch it for you.'

Georgiana smiled slightly. To be able to switch from what their relationship had been to this little re-enactment of marital harmony was strange, to say the least. She watched James going to the desk to fetch her key. He had been tactful on the subject of separate rooms, and had made sure that she had a solo suite overlooking the courtyard, where, once it became too hot for walking, she would return and have a siesta on a balconied chair.

She watched him climbing the stairs to the upper floors. He had never seemed taller than he did now in Italy; part of the tradition of tall, visiting Englishmen that the Italians had recognised and respected since the early eighteenth century. She closed her eyes, and tried to imagine what Dr McCulloch would say if he could see her now? 'What, not run away yet?' No, not yet, but soon, soon; once they got to Stranragh's villa, and he was safely involved in some new routine. Planning a new part of the garden, or something, she thought vaguely, anything that would keep his mind off her for some part of the day, then she would go; and this time she *would* take Jennifer's advice and leave a note upon the chimney-piece.

'There you are.'

He placed the cardigan tenderly around her shoulders, and looked down at her with concern.

'You are feeling all right?'

'Yes, of course, fine. Why?'

'Nothing. You look a little pale, that's all.'

'I was just feeling a little strange,' she said truthfully. 'As if something was about to happen.'

Stranragh didn't reply. Georgiana walked ahead of him out into the sunshine. He watched her small perfectly formed body. Never, since the day he had first fallen in love with her nude form in an oil painting, had he felt so impassioned by her, he thought. He did not question whether or not she had forgiven him, for he knew that he was more sinned against than sinning, and that whatever had passed between them in anger and bitterness must now retreat. Georgiana might have failed him as a lover or a wife, but as a mother her ancestry alone was enough to make her ideal.

This morning he was taking her to see the Giotto 'Madonna with Angels' in the Uffizi. It would be very appropriate, for she was not a cosy figure, by no means a Madonna with Apple, a mother of roundness and warmth ready to pick up her baby and breastfeed him at any moment, but a Madonna of Majesty, with a small king on her knee. Her grave aristocratic expression stared out at the onlooker, in no doubt at all that it was God's son who was sitting upon her knee. Around her knelt a tenantry of angels and attendants. Stranragh put on his

Herbert Johnson hat and caught Georgiana up as she waited to cross the road.

'I think you're going to like this,' he said, as they walked along, and as he had done every morning for the past week.

'Yes,' said Georgiana. Then realising that she sounded a little too uninterested she added, 'I do like Florence. It has such a lovely atmosphere, as if the Renaissance, as you said the other day, as if the Renaissance had only just happened.'

Stranragh nodded approvingly. She was beginning to show signs, in her conversation, of intelligence and appreciation. It was exciting to see that it was possible, after all, to change her. She was not just the social butterfly that his step-mother feared her to be.

The streets they passed were dark and cool in places; and sometimes Georgiana would stop dutifully in some doorway and point out a scene 'just like that painting you showed me'. When she did this James would nod briskly, and make to move on. He liked to think of her appreciation deepening, but not developing without him.

It was in one of these little dark archways, where Georgiana had stopped to admire a workshop fashioning small flowers out of metal, that she bought a rose. Stranragh could not see its appeal, but since it was inexpensive he bought it for her, and then having paid for it, he stood himself to watch the artisans at work. He said it reminded him of 'The Land'. Georgiana did not know the poem, so drifted back into the street. The fire from inside made the heat of the outside seem cool. She liked these little wanderings of theirs that they took on

127

the way to somewhere else, much more than their eventual destinations.

She unwrapped the rose from its piece of black tissue paper and stuck the little sticky ribbon that had fastened it to her tourist guide. For a few minutes she stood twirling her gift beneath her nose, as if it were a real long-stemmed rose sent to her by a lover.

The street was empty and she became absorbed by its atmosphere. The sunshine, the grey stone, the arched doorways. She was in that happy state of being idle, yet occupied, when she saw a man carrying a parcel emerge from a door opposite. He stood with his back to her. Tall, dark-haired, he was thanking a small Italianate gentleman dressed in a paint-splashed apron who was obviously known to him, for he hugged him several times, causing his companion to stoop laughingly to allow this demonstration of affection. Then he turned, or half-turned, and Georgiana shrank back into the darkened doorway. She watched terrified lest he should see her, as he crossed the road and, walking with that familiar, quick, light step of his, passed her.

In all the months during which they had had their affair, it had never once occurred to Georgiana that Augustus Hackett Esq was handsome. Now, as he passed her, standing in her welcome shadows, she saw that he was. It wasn't just his tanned face and his faded denim shirt, or the cool green eyes and the high forehead, it was his aura. He had an aura of confidence and appeal of the kind that she had once had, before she married James. And he looked as if he had no longer any need of anyone.

'Georgiana?'

She turned.

'Ah, there you are. Are you all right?'

Georgiana stared up at James, suddenly aware that his voice was echoing, very English, very Eton, down the warm quiet street. If he had been speaking Italian, perhaps Gus would not have turned, but people always do turn when they hear their own language, however often, when they're walking alone and in a foreign street.

And then her name was not as ordinary as it might be. Even Gus, whose address book had always throbbed with the names of girls going back as far as when he was at the Slade, even he could not have had so many affairs with a Georgiana that it would not arouse his curiosity. And so, because he heard James's voice, or because he heard her name, he turned and saw them standing there.

'Walk on,' she wanted to say, 'please don't see me.'

And yet she knew it was his right, for he had loved her and she had deceived him. And she had left him, so she deserved for him to see her now, her beauty gone, her charm vanished. She stood a little way behind James as both men talked, pulling at her cardigan as if she was hoping that it would disguise her. Gus himself seemed unsurprised to see them in Florence. But then he had always had a way of seeming unsurprised. He only seemed interested in whether or not they'd been to 'the house' and seen his paintings.

'I finished them quite a while ago,' he told Stranragh. 'I think you'll like them.'

'I'm sure I shall.'

'I'm still staying near Lucca.'

Georgiana was now doing up all the buttons on her cardigan, very slowly and meticulously.

'Good. Then come to lunch.'

'Fine.'

'How about Sunday? We'll have been settled in a few days by then.'

'May I bring—'

'Bring whoever you wish,' said Stranragh graciously. 'Any time after midday. We'll be lunching by the pool.'

James raised his hand briefly in a small gesture and Georgiana smiled vaguely past it.

'Aren't you going to be hot like that?' asked Gus as he prepared to walk off.

Georgiana looked down at her cardigan which was now buttoned tightly round her.

'She feels the cold a great deal at the moment,' said James, answering for her. 'Even here. You know how it is when women are pregnant.'

Gus smiled again.

'Happily no,' he said.

They raised hands again in gestures of parting and James walked on up the street with Georgiana following, her cardigan still buttoned tightly round her.

No-one can re-meet a lover with the cool that is necessary. In the imagination such reunions are surrounded by an acceptance of former physical intimacies that is simply not present in life. Mouths form 'good mornings', and 'how are yous', and 'do you knows', but eyes say 'you know what I'm like', 'you remember when', 'have you forgotten that afternoon?' Gus's gaze, half-amused, wholly impudent, had been unavoidable. He had mocked her cardigan because he was, she knew,

130

mocking her respectable façade. And he had asked himself to lunch with someone else to show Georgiana that she was part of the past, a place where she had once held power, but where he no longer stayed. 'It's been quite spoilt, you know, we no longer go there.'

Of course James had had to mention her pregnancy; that was his way of telling Gus that he was 'occupying' Georgiana. It was his ensign that flew above her. Staring obediently up at the 'Madonna with Angels', Georgiana found herself hating this gracious symbol of motherhood, with her rather self-possessed baby who would no doubt be immensely improved once there was someone besides himself in the nursery. She had deceived Gus into thinking she was married, and now she was deceiving James into thinking she was pregnant. What would Nanny say?

'Can we go to lunch?'

James frowned. He was in the middle of his most interesting observational comparison.

'It's the baby – it's making me feel hungry,' said Georgiana, and then had the honesty to blush.

'Then of course.'

James removed his 'lecture tour' horn-rimmed glasses, and protectiveness overcoming his disappointment in being interrupted during one of his favourite pieces, he took her to lunch in a restaurant that he knew, and to which he had not yet taken her.

It would have been perfect, with someone else. Trees to sit under, white wine at exactly the right temperature, light delicate pasta dishes, the herbs freshly picked, the sauces lightly made, little baby vegetables crisply served, but Georgiana detested it, with all the manic

131

hatred that a girl feels when she has been shamed by someone.

James didn't notice anything, or if he did, he was too courteous to comment. For now that he thought their story was working out so calmly and respectably, James was almost courtly. He made up for her lack of conversation by continuing his lecture on Giotto. Georgiana thought that if he had been a dress designer it might have made her just a tiny bit more interested; but as it was, she sat there in her hated cardigan, her cotton 'frock' (there was no other word for what she was wearing) and her sensible shoes for 'rubbernecking' as James called sightseeing, and wished that she was somewhere else.

It wasn't difficult to get James to allow her to return to the hotel early for her siesta, and while he strolled back to the Uffizi, still immersed in, and admiring of, his own erudition, Georgiana lay on a chair under a canopy and stared down at the courtyard below.

She had seen herself, her new self, through Gus's eyes, and she had hated it. He used to point out people like herself and laugh at them, and although she had laughed too, she hadn't been able to see the joke until now. And the joke was there *was* no joke, *they* were the joke, Gus's joke.

'You're so predictable,' he used to say, and he had said it again today as he had said of her cardigan, 'aren't you going to be hot like that?'

What he was really saying was that he always knew that they'd end up meeting in a place like Florence, a couple of years after their affair, and that she would be wearing a cardigan and sensible shoes, and she would be thinner (he hated thin women); and beside her would be a tall sensible husband, and they would exchange small talk and maybe meet 'for drinks' or 'for lunch', and then pass on their way, she rejoicing in her conformity, he rejoicing in the accuracy of his prediction.

But she wasn't rejoicing in her conformity, and she didn't like the person she had become, or was about to become, and it had nothing to do with Stranragh or their marriage, but everything to do with her. When, at nineteen, she had run away from Mary's house and gone to live with her first lover, for just a few weeks, she had been happy. But Kaminski had left her, possibly because he knew, as Gus had seemed to know, that it would not, could not, be long before she reverted to type. Kaminski the sophisticated had left her in that mature and tactful way she now recognised that men always left girls of nineteen, once they had enjoyed them.

Shadows crept across the courtyard, reaching out for each other and eventually touching. Georgiana watched them without moving, as she had as a child.

At dinner that night James talked about Hackett. He seemed to enjoy it. He was a good painter, he thought, but he wondered whether he'd ever make it. They both knew that he'd 'made' Georgiana, but as with so many of his sex, it seemed that James was unafraid of the past. Or perhaps it was that looking at what he thought was a pregnant Georgiana, he felt no need to be anything but assured. With evident relish he told her about Hackett's long supply of local girls and the way he used them as models for his Biblical scenes; he described how the housekeeper had been visited in protest by the local priest who departed reassured, it seemed, by the 'holy' nature of the frescoes on the walls. Georgiana pretended amusement. James was looking forward to taking her to the house: she had only seen pictures of it, but they did not do it justice, he told her, it was more beautiful than that.

And it was. As they drove slowly up through the avenue of trees, Georgiana imagined Gus arriving there, and how he would have stood back admiring it, and how he would have walked about looking for ways to criticize it, and been unable to find any. The soft stone, the avenues and vistas, the hills behind – even Gus must have been pleased, although he would not have said so.

The frescoes in the hall (or atrium, as James correctly called it) were charming. Anything to do with the Bible was not first on Georgiana's list of interests, but Gus, once commissioned by the low-church Stranragh to paint scenes from the Good Book, had turned the chosen subjects into celebrations of life's joys, and as in the frescoes that she had seen in Florence the faces were the faces of the people who lived hereabouts. Even the priest (obviously won firmly round to this artistic enterprise) was seen busily teaching in a corner of the Temple.

Feminine beauty, Gus's abiding passion, was abundant. As Georgiana stared round the walls, she wondered idly which of the nubile beauties staring at her from the walls would accompany Gus to lunch on Sunday.

The night before she sent the housekeeper to say that she felt unwell and wouldn't be down. She felt no guilt at this, for she knew that in many ways James preferred to sit with a book propped up against a bottle of wine and read his way through dinner. And for herself, she missed nothing, but sat watching the garden and the insects circling the lamps.

When Hackett, as James insisted on calling him, arrived, it was as if the house started to reverberate. He brought with him a colossal energy and a kind of vibrancy that was so different from Stranragh. It was as if a jazz group was drowning a minuet: Stranragh's smooth Etonian tones, Hackett's Brentford-tinged baritone.

She watched them from her balcony as they strolled round the garden. Naturally Gus had brought with him a beautiful girl, not dark as Georgiana had expected, but blonde, with long fair hair that reached down to her waist. She must have been about eighteen or nineteen, but looked only fifteen. It was not surprising to see Gus with yet another beautiful girl, in fact it would have been strange had he not been accompanied by someone so lovely. He had impeccable taste in women, and because women fascinated him, he had no trouble fascinating them. He was not a womaniser so much as a womanophile, if there was such a thing, thought Georgiana wryly, and then she retreated from her hiding place and lay on her bed.

It was not difficult being 'ill'. She had thought of herself as unwell for so long now that she was quite able to lie down and feel unable to get up. She did this with gratitude to her frailty, because she knew that she would have hated to see Gus sitting at lunch with a decorative companion, someone younger than she. And he would take such delight, she imagined, in the situation – he free and loving life, she stuck with James, a man who was so dull and so pompous, a man so exactly like the man that she had invented as a husband while they were having their affair.

She imagined them all lunching under the trees, picturing the dappled Impressionistic scene, the food set upon the heavy white linen cloth, the green glasses decorated with grapes that James always used outside, the locally-made plates decorated with flowers and leaves. And then she shut her eyes and went to sleep.

Most people wake when they know they are being watched. They wake as if they know instinctively that sleep is a private and intimate affair, a function to be followed alone and unobserved. Georgiana thought she awoke because of the heat, because it must be mid-afternoon, and often by mid-afternoon she would find rest impossible, and it was her habit to take a cold shower at that time. Now she awoke because Gus was in her room staring at her.

She sat up as he put his finger to his lips. She wanted to say 'what are you doing here?' but she stared at him instead. He sat down on the bed and stared back at her, and for a minute they both said nothing. Then he looked her over critically, before whispering.

'You look terrible.'

'Thank you.'

'What's wrong with you?'

'Oh, you know—' She shrugged her shoulders.

'You used to be so beautiful.'

She turned away from him and looked out of the window. Nothing had changed. He was still Gus, rude and impossible; and when he wasn't being rude and impossible, he was being difficult, and for reasons that she couldn't even begin to understand.

'What's *wrong* with you? I mean, pregnant women,' he shook his head as if he were an expert on them, 'pregnant women are meant to bloom.'

He had given up any attempt at whispering now, and took a packet of cigarettes out of the top pocket of his denim jacket. She hated anyone smoking in her bedroom, but she knew from experience that there was very little point in saying anything to him, and in a way she was afraid to, because the chances were that he would ignore her, or talk so loudly that James would come up.

'Well, aren't they?'

'Aren't they what?'

'Aren't they meant to bloom?'

'Who?'

'Pregnant women.'

'Oh, I don't know. Hadn't you better go? You'll be missed.'

There was a long silence during which Gus got up from her bed, leaving it feeling oddly light, and walked to the window to stare out towards the hills.

'I had to see you.'

He always sounded a great deal more Brentford when he actually meant something.

'Why? There's nothing to see.'

'It's as I say, because you looked so terrible in the street the other day.'

'People do.' Georgiana shrugged again.

'Really? Watcha been doing since I last saw you – taking a course in philosophy?'

'All right, now you've seen me, isn't that enough?'

'No,' said Gus simply.

Georgiana sighed. He had always tired her out with his restless energy, and now he was going to be sincere, which was even more tiring.

'I know you thought you were being clever when – when you were pretending to have a husband, and you didn't – and I can't pretend it didn't cut me up, right? And I can't pretend I'm not glad you're well and truly married now to that boring bastard Stranragh, because boy is he boring, but at the same time, I don't like to see you like this, you know. It does things to me.'

'I'm sorry.'

'Typical. What you sorry about?'

'Whatever it is you're getting so cross about.'

Gus sighed and stubbed his cigarette out in a geranium pot.

'Look, if you don't mind, don't go too near the window.'

'You're not scared of that boring bastard, are you?'

'Yes,' said Georgiana truthfully.

'What's the matter? He beat you up, or something.'

'Yes.'

'Trust you to marry someone who beats you up.'

'He's only done it once.'

'Oh well, there's nothing to worry about then, is there?'

'So – that's that.'

There was a long pause, and then Gus looked down at Georgiana ruefully.

'I feel like Robert Browning visiting Elizabeth Barrett, with you like that.'

Georgiana smiled.

'I look worse than I am.'

'You look terrible. I just can't believe you're pregnant. How many months?' His voice assumed its normal baritone. 'I mean how many months are you meant to be up the spout?'

'Shsh.'

'I will not shsh. Pregnant women,' he leant forward, 'for a start, pregnant women, their breasts change shape.'

Georgiana hated the way Gus always said breasts. It was real in a way that she didn't like, in the way that her marriage had turned out to be real.

'Well, m'lady?'

'Please don't keep calling me that.'

'Why?'

'Oh, I don't know, because I don't like it, I suppose.'

He looked at her and then sighed.

'I still haven't got over you – you know that? I don't know why.'

'You've had enough girlfriends.'

'Yes,' he agreed, 'I do seem to have done half the neighbourhood.'

'I hear the priest was after you.'

'He's all right. He's done the other half.' He frowned. 'How about you? You had any lovers, after me?'

'No, just a marriage. A bit of a marriage.'

'That's all right then.'

He sat down on the bed again.

'Doesn't it mean anything that I – that I haven't forgotten you?'

Georgiana nodded, and then they stopped talking and he kissed her.

'My God,' said Gus, amazed, 'you still love me.'

'Shsh – *whisper*.'

'Oh he can go to hell.'

'No, you must, or he'll come up.'

'Forget him. He's not important.'

He shook her by the arms, and then looked at them.

'Christ, your arms are thin.'

Georgiana crossed them self-consciously.

'You always complained about them.'

'Did I?'

'You hated painting them—'

'Look, you're coming away with me.'

'I can't.'

'Yes you can.'

'When?'

'Now. When the hell do you think?'

'What about that girl, your girl downstairs?'

Gus laughed.

'You can't just leave her,' said Georgiana, 'I mean—'

'She's a nymphomaniac.'

'She can't be, she looks so innocent—'

'The neighbourhood is crawling with them. Must be something in the water.'

He stood up.

'Coming?'

'Gus, I can't.'

She got off her bed and stood looking up at him in her bare feet.

'Come on. Don't make an opera out of it.'

'I—'

'Put your shoes on like a good girl, and we're off.'

'I haven't packed my suitcase. I haven't told James.'

Gus took his packet of cigarettes out of the top pocket of his denim jacket and tapped it expertly.

'You've got two minutes to make up your mind.'

He lit the cigarette, and then rolled it to the side of his mouth before withdrawing it.

'By the time I've reached the end of this cigarette. Actually, to be fair, probably slightly longer than two minutes.'

Georgiana stared up at him. If he had tried to make love to her, or pleaded with her, it might have been easier, but because he was Gus, he just looked down at her, mocking the conventional struggle that was taking place within her.

'Is it so difficult?' he asked after a minute.

'No, that's just it, it's too easy.'

'Well then, come on.'

'But where shall we – go?'

'To my house. You'll like it.'

'But how shall we live?'

He started to laugh.

'Do you know, one of the things that I love about you is – you're such a little materialist.'

'We have to think of these things.'

'Why?' he mocked.

Georgiana stood back from him.

'I really should tell James.'

'Tell James, don't tell James, but get going.'

'But I don't want to.'

'Why ever not? You don't love him, do you?'

'No, no, I was going anyway, just as soon – I was going. No, it's just that last time I told him – it wasn't very pleasant.'

She couldn't explain to Gus how utterly lacking in any kind of courage she had been. She couldn't explain anything, because she wasn't very good at talking about her feelings, and because she was afraid he would laugh at the things she had found so serious and would find, as doubtless she soon would anyway, that all her sufferings and her fears had been unnecessary.

Looking at her standing there, still barefooted and even tinier than he remembered her, Gus sighed. They had known each other and loved each other in such different ways before. He because he had enjoyed the idea of laying a bit of Old England, and she because she had had to lay the ghost of a previous affair; but now it was different. He knew now that he loved her in a way that changes a man, takes his life and transposes it to another key. He knew she wanted him to tell her, like a child, that everything was going to be all right, that everyone would live happily ever after.

'I will take care of you, you know.'

'Yes. I think you will.'

'Hackett? Hackett?'

It was Stranragh's voice calling from below her balcony. Georgiana stiffened.

'Oh my God,' she whispered.

She went to the balcony.

'We've lost Hackett,' said James.

Georgiana stared down at him. Would she always feel grateful to him for calling to her now? Would she know now that this thing that she was contemplating, this desertion, was wrong? Staring down into James's face would she see not someone she had learned to loathe, but a man whom she had in fact destroyed? And knowing this, would she also know that she could not now leave him for this perhaps worthless passion? Husbands so often turned out to be decent and loving, and lovers so often the opposite. She had been brought up to the idea that you could learn to love someone, that marriage somewhere within your class was as indispensable as oxygen. Well, she had tried it, and it was terrible. Terrible in ways that no-one ever told you about when they were lecturing you on the subject. As if marriage was a pair of stately gates through which you passed never to suffer again.

'You haven't seen him, have you?' asked James.

'Yes,' Georgiana heard herself saying, 'yes, he's here.'

'What's he doing there?'

Georgiana felt quite sorry for James, standing there, staring up at her.

'He's making love to me. No. Not making love, kissing. At least he has been.'

'What on earth would he want to do that for?'

Georgiana suddenly hated James more than ever. He saw himself as some kind of ideal Englishman, so unflapped by everything, when in reality, she knew he was something else.

Gus now joined her, and leant over the balcony.

'Is this true, Hackett?'

Gus nodded.

'Yes, I was just kissing her.'

He made it sound as if he was referring to a practice that any guest enjoyed after lunch.

'Yes, just kissing her,' he said again, 'but now I'm going, and she's coming with me.'

'Are you tight, Hackett?'

'No,' said Gus, 'but I probably will be this evening.'

They passed him in the hall. As they passed, James said to Georgiana, 'If you go now, I'll hound you for the rest of your days.'

Gus stopped.

'Isn't that typical? She's a *woman*, Stranragh, not a fox.'

Stranragh moved towards Georgiana as if to hit her, but Gus pushed him away.

'You remind me of a guy at school. Used to beat up boys' sisters to get his own back. Been to all the right schools, and that's what they taught you, is it?'

Stranragh looked at Hackett. Perhaps because he was more casually dressed, he seemed taller and more muscular. He revenged himself by turning to Gus's lunch companion and telling her, in Italian, what was happening. As Gus drove away, she ran after the car and threw a stone. Gus put his foot down and the dust from the road flew around the car. He started to sing a snatch from *The Barber of Seville*, something he always did when he was in a particularly good mood. Georgiana stared ahead. There was a pleasant simplicity to everything suddenly. The road stretched ahead, reddish and winding steeply. They passed domestic Sunday sights. Women clearing tables while men slept, children playing.

'You're not really pregnant, are you? I mean, I don't mind, but you're not, are you?'

'No.'

'I thought you weren't,' he said, and then he turned and looked at her. 'Don't worry, I'll soon change that.'

# 7

Clarissa Gillott, presently still (alas) the wife of the Hon Andrew Gillott, was entertaining the Countess to tea, although entertaining was not the word that the Countess would have used for it. She had put out her best Royal Albert (rose design) china and her best silver teapot (Edwardian plated), and had employed a woman from the village in a green nylon overall to open the door to the Countess. Alas, none of this had really worked on the Countess as it should, for she was used to using a Wedgwood service for every day and hated anything but eighteenth-century silver.

Clarissa passed her a bowl of lump sugar with the tongs. The Countess ignored the tongs, picked up one lump and plopped it in her teacup. She then watched it sink slowly, with such interest that an onlooker might have been forgiven for thinking that she expected it to re-emerge at the surface again and float about gaily like an indiarubber ball. There had been little conversation. The Countess had not encouraged it. Now she looked out of Clarissa's window on to the lawn where the October leaves were just beginning to collect into little groups.

Seeing the Countess's gaze directed towards her garden, Clarissa sought frantically to remember some rare shrub or flower that she could introduce as a topic.

Her eye alighted on a pink Japanese anemone which her gardener (four days a month) had informed her had a very pleasing shape.

'I see you're looking at the Japanese anemone,' she said brightly. 'So nice to have something this time of year.'

The Countess didn't reply but stared out of the window, if anything, even more intensely. It was as if she could see something that Clarissa couldn't.

'It's got such a pretty habit,' Clarissa went on. 'I do so love to have new flowering things this time of year. I mean if you have everything for spring and summer then there's nothing left for – autumn,' she added helplessly.

Clarissa stopped talking. Even she realised that her small range of topics was not having the desired effect of eliciting a response from her guest. She lapsed into gazing instead, with a magpie's interest, at the Countess's jewellery. She herself had jewellery, of course, but she did not have gems. The Countess had gems, large gems that flashed and caught the light. Gems that spoke of the British in India, and 'look what Bertie gave me'. They were quite magnificent, and Clarissa would have loved to try them on. She particularly fancied herself in the large emerald ring, and she saw herself clasping the matching brooch to the lapel of her good navy-blue gaberdine suit. It would be a wonderful thing to go to lunch somewhere with someone (she couldn't for the moment imagine who), wearing gems such as the Countess was sporting. She saw herself in them, perhaps sitting in a bay window lunching at the Ritz, the light catching them so vividly that there would be no need whatsoever to catch the eye of the waiter.

Now the Countess's gaze turned on Clarissa. Her green eyes had a hooded look, matching the falcon on her small green-stoned signet ring.

'You have heard, of course?' she asked.

Clarissa rattled her teacup, quite by mistake. She had heard, of course, but whether or not she should admit to hearing was quite another matter. She replaced her teacup carefully, for judging from the 'constant drain' (as she called Andrew) on her finances of late, there would not be a great deal of extra money to spend on new sets of Royal Albert.

'I am sure you must have heard,' said the Countess.

Clarissa's feet, shod in a new pair of Russell and Bromley's best and most tasteful shoes, shifted uneasily. She smoothed her divided skirt over her knees.

'I had heard something,' she admitted.

'Of course you have,' said the Countess, barely bothering to cover her impatience with the silly woman. 'Of course you have. The girls have been friends for years, since school, I believe.'

She was just about to add thoughtlessly that 'girls' always made such funny friends at school, when she realised, just in the nick of time, that if she wanted 'the Gillott woman' to be of use to her, she had to refrain from treating her in quite the same way that she would have normally, so to speak.

'They've known each other since childhood,' was how she put it, after a pause, 'and so that is why I am here today.'

147

'I see,' said Clarissa, and her self-importance became immediately all too evident. 'I thought as much.'

The Countess sighed inwardly, once more. The trouble with the middle class was that they were so – middle class. Give them an inch and they would hire a social secretary and start putting themselves down for Whites. It was tedious to deal with, but it had to be done.

'Yes, I expect you did,' said the Countess with a small attempt at being gracious.

'I realised,' Clarissa's hands smoothed her new silk blouse over her arms and pointedly re-adjusted her gold charm bracelet over the cuff, 'that your visit would be not, let us say, unconnected with Georgiana. It must be ghastly for you.'

The Countess's gaze redirected itself once more out of the drawing-room window and towards the leaf-littered lawn. She could willingly wring Georgiana's neck, not least for putting her through this dreadful embarrassment of having to ask the assistance of a woman whom she heartily disliked. But a scandal was a scandal, and the Countess had no love for scandals that were connected to her. Other people's were perfectly enjoyable, but not your own, or those of anyone connected to you, and she had to make every effort, but every single effort she could, to get Georgiana back to Stranragh, and Stranragh to come to his senses and let her live in London, or wherever it was that she wished.

In some ways, she realised, it had been completely Stranragh's fault, although there would be no earthly good in telling him so, for he had behaved in a very silly way with a girl so much younger than himself. In short, he had expected to go on living in Scotland in the same

148

way as he had as a bachelor. A typical member of his sex, quite obviously; but unfortunately he had married her niece, and it was the Countess's clear duty to get them both back together again, living in the kind of detached harmony that was normal for persons such as themselves. It would not be difficult for them to do so, not once the baby was born, for babies had a wonderful way of taking a girl's mind off things like love that didn't matter a fig, and concentrating them on the essentials of life, such as putting him down for Eton, or whatever, and going out and about in a civilized manner.

'It is not very pleasant,' the Countess agreed, her eyeline still fixed firmly on the exterior, 'but then, so much of life isn't, is it?'

'No, absolutely ghastly,' said Clarissa with a great deal of feeling. 'So much that is *so* ghastly. Every paper you pick up has something ghastly. Ghastly things, even about the Royals.'

The Countess shuddered inwardly. Mrs Gillott would, would she not, refer to the first family as 'the Royals'. It would be a term of reference that she would pick up *just like that.*

'Jennifer was appalled,' said Clarissa, 'at Georgiana's *appearance.* I mean when she came down on the visit, she thought, well she thought the marriage was not going at all well, but then, she wasn't *pregnant* then. I mean I would have thought that would make such a difference, to a – gel,' Clarissa ended triumphantly, having, she felt, pronounced it so terribly well that even the Countess must have noticed. (She was having trouble with 'goff' and 'otel' but no doubt they would, one day very soon, arrive; and, she hoped, as effortlessly as 'gel' just had.)

149

'I think,' said the Countess, ignoring everything that Clarissa had just said but redirecting her gaze straight at her, 'I think that Jennifer could help Georgiana come to her senses. In fact, I am quite sure she can. She, after all, is a mother now. She can explain to Georgiana the delights of motherhood, once the children are safely provided for, and you can have a nanny and a small staff to help you.'

'I think that sounds a very sensible idea,' said Clarissa, her tone changing to the one that she used for chairing the meetings of the village Mixed Fruit and Veg Society. 'A very good idea. Most beneficial to both of them. Good for Jennifer to have to do something positive for once, instead of sitting around all the time just having babies. Oh yes. A very good idea.'

'But will she do it?' asked the Countess. 'She may take the line,' and there was no doubt from the Countess's tone that in her opinion it would be the wrong line, 'she may take the line that she must not interfere in someone else's life. May she not?'

'Not if I have anything to do with it,' said Clarissa quickly, her dislike for her daughter creeping all too obviously into her voice. 'That would be silly.'

'Of course it would be silly, but nevertheless, she might. She may even sympathize with Georgiana in her present straits.'

'*That* would be silly.'

'Of course, but she might.'

'What line do *you* think she'll take?'

Clarissa was naturally loath to tell the Countess that whatever line she told Jennifer to take, or not to take, she would be sure to take the opposite point of view.

Instead of admitting this basic weakness in her maternal influence, she offered the Countess a further cup of tea, and was accepted.

'One does see,' continued the Countess, 'that the young must stick together, or think they must, but, on the other hand, Jennifer is a sensible person, at least one would gather that from her appearance, I should have thought; and a sensible person will, I think, never persuade another person of anything that will not be to their absolute benefit, and it would not be of absolute benefit, I think we would all agree, for Georgiana to spend the rest of her days with a Monsieur Dubedat.'

Clarissa was in total accord with everything that the Countess had just opined, but now she allowed herself a small frown. 'But I thought his name was Hackett.'

'Dubedat was a painter in – well, never mind that. What I mean is, painters have not the reputation for making persons such as Georgiana happy.'

'I only like dead painters because their paintings are worth so much more,' agreed Clarissa. 'I bought a watercolour the other day from the Country Living Gallery, I don't know whether you noticed it in the Hall? A lovely little thing called "Mummy's Best Friend"?'

'No,' said the Countess firmly. Her late, very great husband used to turn people out of the house if they mentioned his 'things' (as he referred to his paintings) and so on; and would walk out of theirs if they drew attention to anything they owned. And how right he was, she thought, for two of the worst conversation killers that had crept into customary use over the past two decades were money and possessions. How dull they were. Infinitely and endlessly dull, drawing attention as they did to people's baseness and greed. That everyone was base, and greedy, was a foregone conclusion, but that conversation of all things should turn itself towards this, and highlight the very aspects that it should be covering, was most unappealing.

And as for Mrs Gillott's purchase of an overpriced watercolour from some fearful little gallery, sporting no doubt faked Victorian pictures of children feeding their rabbits or holding dollies' tea parties, why, the idea of being able to dredge up one word to say about it was ludicrous. She looked across at Mrs Gillott. It had been a miracle that she had been able to persuade Andrew to marry her, for she was a dreadfully plain woman. Not that her features were necessarily repulsive, for all in all, taken one by one, they could be thought to be quite pretty. No doubt a few years ago she *had* been thought pretty, but now, putting her features back together again, the whole face was dominated by this macabre mercantile soul. Mrs Gillott would not see the hilarity in social pretensions, she would only see the importance of them. She would not revere the old values because they were the walls within which certain unpleasantnesses could be contained, she would only assess them in order to advance herself. She could not take her marriage to an old buffoon like Gillott with a pinch of salt, she would take it, as she took everything, as a reflection on herself. She was quite appalling.

'So,' the Countess pulled herself to her feet, her use of the sofa arm almost undetectable, for she disdained a stick for her increasing arthritis, 'I can count on you to exert your influence on Jennifer? She's a good girl,

I think. She has caused you no – heartaches. I'm sure she will be an influence for the good on Georgiana.'

Clarissa wished that she had the Countess's certainty. Ever since Jennifer had married Pemberton she had become very much her own person, as any girl will who is the mistress of five houses, seven cars, fifteen racehorses, and an art collection which could be kindly loaned. (Part of it was currently on show in 'English Country Houses As They Were', which was a source of some pain to Clarissa, and one of the reasons for the purchase of the watercolour for the Hall.)

'Tell Jennifer,' the Countess paused by the front door, 'tell Jennifer that if she does this, she will make me very happy.'

Clarissa wondered fleetingly, if making the Countess happy was going to mean a great deal to Jennifer, but then she thought it might, because only the other day Jennifer had let slip that the Countess had not agreed with what she was doing in the garden, and had been most outspoken on the subject; so, perhaps, after all, Jennifer could be persuaded to influence Georgiana to go back to her husband, and then the Countess would be nice about the alterations she had made in the garden, and that would make Jennifer happy.

Clarissa was so preoccupied by her increasing power that she forgot to call Mrs Miller from the kitchen to open the front door. She had opened it herself before the thought for which she was searching clarified itself in her mind. What was *she* going to get out of this arrangement? Supposing she was able to persuade Jennifer to persuade Georgiana to leave this wretched painter and return to her husband, what would she, personally, get out of it, for all her pains? The Countess, after all, was in part responsible for her marriage to Andrew, for Andrew had told her that she had 'approved', which at the time had seemed most exciting; and now that Andrew was proving such a personal and financial liability, it would be only right, and in the circumstances fair, for the Countess to help Clarissa off-load him.

'I was wondering,' said Clarissa, as she opened the Countess's car door for her, 'I was wondering if you could do something for me?'

For the first time in the whole hour and a quarter the Countess looked openly embarrassed. To be as quickly obvious as Mrs Gillott was daunting.

But there are two kinds of people, as her mother used to say. One kind who in response to 'can you?' says 'it depends what it is', and the other who says 'of course'.

'Of course.'

'Could *you* perhaps encourage Andrew to take a trip somewhere? You know in the old days he was always so intrepid, so much the brave explorer, but now he's really such a stay-at-home, and I don't think it's good for him.'

'Of course.' The Countess lowered herself into her seat and swung her legs elegantly into the car. 'As a matter of fact he was saying to me only the other day that he felt a little, shall we say, "hemmed in" – of course a trip would do him good.'

Clarissa did not at all like the idea that her husband was confiding in anyone about being hemmed in or anything else. She shut the car door loudly and stood back. The Countess lowered her window and leant out, for quite obviously another thought had occurred.

'As a matter of fact, a friend of mine is organising something rather amusing, to China. You know, a sort of cultural exchange of ideas, basically, but mixing in some fun as well. Apparently the Chinese are very interested in reproducing many of our antiques to export to America – we have so much really fine Chinoiserie which of course *they* all smashed during the Revolution. Andrew would be just the person to go along as a courier. You know, he's quite an expert, and of course he does speak old Chinese, which isn't a great deal of good nowadays, but it's better than nothing.'

She wound the window up again, and within a very short space of time the car had turned into the road and disappeared from sight, leaving Clarissa with those mixed feelings that always result from someone supplying you with information about your nearest and dearest of which, until that moment, you have been entirely ignorant. The idea of Andrew being an expert on Chinese, or even speaking it, was so entirely foreign that for a moment she felt the Countess must have been referring to someone else. And then she felt that he had been unfaithful to her in some way. That he had been holding back secrets in an effort to deceive her. By the time she had closed the front door Andrew's ability to speak Chinese had become as vile to her as if she had discovered a previous wife he had failed to mention.

She went back into the drawing room and sat down, breathing heavily. The 'constant drain' was away in London on his twentieth visit to his dentist. She often wondered how it was that the dentist ever managed to do any fillings for Andrew, for he must have to catch him so quickly between cigarettes that even the high speed drill would be hard put to do its work in the required time. She imagined Andrew, a cigarette in one hand, a copy of the *Life* heavily marked with the day's bets in the other, sitting in the waiting room. The other patients might cough pointedly and nod at the 'No Smoking' notice; he would merely open the window and puff his smoke outwards. Clarissa shuddered. It was terrible to think of Andrew when he wasn't with you, and terrible to think of him when he was. She turned to the telephone and dialled Jennifer's number.

Jennifer did not answer, but Bloss did. Jennifer must therefore be doing her tapestry in a bad mood, or she must be in the nursery in a good mood playing with the children, for normally she answered the telephone at the same time as Bloss, giving the impression that both of them were so bored with the quiet rhythm of life at the Hall that the merest ring of the telephone became a matter of great moment. Not today, however. Today there was just Bloss, and it sounded as if he was sucking a sweet.

'Could I speak to Lady Pemberton, please, Bloss?'

'Yes, of course, Mrs Gillott.'

Bloss always managed to make 'Mrs' sound like a criminal record. As he went to fetch Jennifer, Clarissa mentally practised 'Lady Gillott' and found it a great deal more agreeable. And then she imagined the life she would have at the Hall. Parties of people down every weekend. A chef to cook specially for them, of course, and banks of flowers in every room. Not for her her daughter's hermit existence, and a life spent preoccupied with whether or not someone's tooth had come through, or the woman from the village was putting too much starch in the napkins and charging twopence too much. She really wondered, as she did quite often, whether it was worth being as rich as Jennifer if your whole life was lived on the same level as the people you employed. As a matter of fact, when she thought about it, Bloss had more of a social life down at the Queen's Arms than Jennifer and Pemberton up at the Hall.

'Ah, there you are.'

Jennifer hated the way her mother always said 'ah, there you are' instead of 'hallo', as if whatever time she had taken in coming to the telephone had been too long for her.

'Hallo,' said Jennifer, ignoring her.

'I wondered if you were terribly busy this week?'

Of course they both knew that she wasn't, but a small pretence at Jennifer having some sort of social life had to be made.

'No, as a matter of fact I'm fairly free this week, just a great deal of home organising to do.'

'You've got a staff for that.'

'Yes, I know, but the staff need organizing.'

'I should have – oh well, never mind. May I come over for lunch, then?'

'I don't see why not,' said Jennifer, which Clarissa found rather a funny way of putting it. 'No, I don't see why not at all.'

Clarissa was extremely glad to hear it. She liked lunch at the Hall, not because the food was good, which generally speaking it wasn't, but because at least there was no nonsense with having to help or anything. At least it made a change.

'Very well, shall we say Wednesday, then?'

'I don't see why not,' said Jennifer again, and Clarissa felt justified in saying goodbye rather quickly.

And so to lunch at the Hall with her daughter. The navy-blue gaberdine suit was put out – not, alas, with the kind of gems the Countess sported, but with a small bar brooch with small diamonds posed on it and a single strand of pearls.

Jennifer opened the door, to Clarissa's evident disappointment. Jennifer was in a rather ratty-looking old skirt and a cardigan that looked as if Nanny had started knitting it with every intention of making a hot-water-bottle cover, and then had changed her mind and made it for Jennifer instead.

Clarissa didn't bother to kiss Jennifer. She never did if Bloss was not present to open the door, which she always found mildly insulting.

'Where's Bloss?' she asked unceremoniously.

'It's Wednesday, his half-day.'

'Why make it Wednesday then? I could have made it any other day, I was free all the other days.'

'I thought it would be cosier on our own. With the hostess trolley.'

'I could have made it any other day,' said Clarissa again, and she went ahead of Jennifer, with glorious indifference to protocol and precedence, into the drawing room.

'No, we're not in there,' Jennifer called after her,

'there's no fire in there. No, we're in my little sitting room.'

Clarissa backed out of the drawing room, but not without first noticing that the dust covers were on.

'You never seem to use that room,' she said. 'It does seem a waste.'

'It's not,' snapped Jennifer.

'Where's Bloss, did you say?'

'I told you, it's his half-day.'

Jennifer always gave Bloss his half-day on whatever day her mother visited, because she felt that Bloss spied on them together and reported anything untoward to the Queen's Arms in the evening. She had also seen him smirking once or twice.

At least the fire was lit in the morning room, for the rest of the house was freezing. Clarissa chose the chair nearest to it. Jennifer carefully removed, one by one, all her tapestry wools, and pushed her tapestry frame to the other side of the fireplace. She sat down facing the frame and started to sew a nice bit of gate. Clarissa watched her do this with evident irritation. Jennifer had always been a plain girl, compared to her mother; everyone had always been very kind, but had always remarked 'isn't she the image of Aidan' whom everyone knew, although a devoted father, was as plain as a pikestaff. No-one, least of all Clarissa, had ever expected Jennifer to marry well. Just to get her married had been her highest expectation, but to see her married not just to a titled man, but to a man with a vast fortune, was, to put it mildly, an astonishment. To view her now, therefore, in her old skirt and cardigan, sewing at her tapestry frame for all the world like some old spinster, was, Clarissa thought, plain silly. There was no other word for it. When you could afford things, it was your *duty* to do so.

'Are you warm in your skirt?' she asked.

'Yes, very,' said Jennifer, not looking up. 'It's a wonderful old skirt this, the dogs love it.'

Clarissa shuddered inwardly. The very idea of wearing what was tantamount to a dog blanket when you did not need to was quite horrifying, and she would have issued a stern lecture to Jennifer if she was not so intent on doing her best for the Countess; who in return would put into motion the plan to send the 'constant drain' to China on an extended mission.

So she smiled instead.

'Darling, would it be too ghastly if we had a sherry? The drive you know, dreadful lorries all the way. Gave me such a thirst.'

Jennifer was used to the sudden switch to surface charm that her mother sometimes felt it necessary to display. She went to a small corner cupboard and removed a bottle of not very expensive sherry that she kept for the rare occasions that she entertained Mrs Dupont from the village. (Increasingly rarer since she had discovered what Pember described rather laboriously as 'Dupont's penchant', which was to repeat absolutely every jot of what she heard at the Hall to everyone except the window cleaner, who was mad anyway.) She poured her mother a small sherry.

'Oh lovely, just a thimbleful, just as I like it,' said Clarissa. 'By the way, as I was driving over, I was trying to think of how to describe you and Pember—'

'Pember says "Anciennes Riches", and there are very few left,' said Jennifer, getting there before her mother.

Clarissa abandoned any attempts at being 'smart' and 'charming', neither of which suited her any better than the sherry.

'Anyway,' she said, beginning a new conversation, 'I expect you've heard from Georgiana?'

Jennifer's head bent once more over her tapestry frame. She had known it was going to be one of those days when she awoke that morning and found that the cat had done something frightful in one of Pember's slippers. It had not been funny, simply because it was Pember who had discovered it – too late. And then Nanny had had one of her days when she had told the children not to love Mummy as much as Nanny, and all of them had been 'Nanny's boys' and not even bothered to want to be kissed and cuddled, and now here was her mother for lunch, ready to make mischief.

'The gynaecologist says I'm very well,' said Jennifer, referring to her rapidly increasing waistline.

'Good, that is good,' said Clarissa, and then added pointedly. 'I expect you'll be glad to buy yourself some new maternity clothes.'

'Oh no,' said Jennifer, pulling down her old cardigan, 'I wouldn't waste the money.'

'Back to Georgiana,' said Clarissa. 'She's having a baby, I hear?'

'Yes,' said Jennifer, 'so it seems, although how I simply wouldn't know.'

Clarissa took a rather too large sip of her sherry. Surely this sort of statement was too naïve even for Jennifer?

'What do you mean?'

'You know, because of Stranragh and his – problem.'

'Oh yes, of course,' said Clarissa, her eyes narrowing,

161

her mind racing, and her foot beginning to wave about in an uncontrollable manner. 'Yes, yes, of course, because of his problem. Still, anyway, there it is, or so it seems, and since it is, it would appear that it would be only beneficial to her to return to her husband.'

Jennifer stuck another needle in the gate. It was possibly because she was pregnant, or possibly it was the business of Pember making such a fuss over his slipper, but whichever way it was, she was not in the mood to be in the least conciliatory towards either life or her mother.

'No, no, not really,' she said.

'What do you mean by this?' Clarissa asked, in exactly the same tone that she used to use with Jennifer over a bad report.

'I mean,' said Jennifer slowly, 'that no, I do not think it would be a good idea for Georgiana to return to her husband. No, I do not. I think it would be a bad thing. He is a horrid man who,' she looked up from the gate and, possibly because she was pregnant, and because of the cat, and because she had had such a tiresome time (so she thought afterwards) she said, 'can't do it.'

'I beg your pardon?' said Clarissa, unwittingly releasing a phrase that she knew was not right for the Hall. 'What did you say?'

'I said,' said Jennifer, returning to the gate with added concentration, 'I said he can't do it.'

'That's what I thought. Please. Never—' she started to forbid Jennifer ever to be so vulgar again, when curiosity overcame prudishness and instead she said, 'but how do you know?'

'Because Georgiana told me,' said Jennifer.

'But she's pregnant—'

'Exactly.'

'So she must not have been telling the truth. The "truth" between girls is rarely so.'

'Not at all. Georgiana always tells the truth to me. She can't not, we know too much about each other.'

Clarissa held out her sherry glass for another. Jennifer appeared not to see it, so she was forced to waggle it about in an embarrassing manner until Jennifer, reluctantly it seemed to her, left her tapestry and made her way once more towards the corner cupboard. Clarissa watched her pour the sherry with a great deal of interest. And then she wondered what there was between Jennifer and Georgiana that did not allow for anything but the truth? She sensed an unnerving steel in her daughter that must have arisen from some revelation to which she herself was not privy.

'What do you think the answer is, then?' she asked.

'The baby cannot be Stranragh's,' said Jennifer.

'This makes things very difficult,' said Clarissa, thinking of her promise to the Countess and the Countess's promise to her. The future, which had begun to seem so roseate without the 'constant drain', darkened.

'I don't see why,' said Jennifer. 'She's not with Stranragh any more, so what does it matter if the baby's his – or whose it is, or isn't?'

'Jennifer. It is of great matter who a person's father is, and it always has been.'

'That's not what Pember says. He says that as long as you think *someone* is, that's all that matters.'

Jennifer snipped her wool and stuck her needle in an old velvet needle-cushion. It was time to go to the dining

163

room and find out what Bloss had left them in the hostess trolley.

Clarissa followed Jennifer to the dining room, doing up the buttons of her suit jacket without really thinking of the cold, for once. Supposing everything that Jennifer had said was true? Supposing that Stranragh in fact couldn't do what he ought, to be a father – well, then who could be the father of the baby? She sat down on her dining room chair and allowed Jennifer, by silent consent, to serve her. If Georgiana was having another man's baby, whose could it be? She stared into the smoked mackerel that Jennifer had put in front of her. Somebody perhaps that Jennifer knew? Somebody that they both knew? She looked across at her burgeoning daughter. It must be somebody who was good at getting women pregnant, because it had to have happened between Georgiana's visit and her return to Scotland, or thereabouts. The mackerel started to look peculiarly unattractive. It suddenly seemed so simple. Everything made sense. Jennifer's off-hand manner, the fact that the girls always told the truth to each other, the fact that Jennifer had, one could almost say, got a lot harder suddenly. Georgiana must have got pregnant by Pemberton.

'Oh, my poor darling,' she said.

'What's wrong? Something wrong with the fish?' asked Jennifer.

'No wonder you look so upset in that old skirt.'

'What on earth are you talking about?' asked Jennifer. 'This old skirt, as you refer to it, is a St Laurent.' She didn't add, 'Which is a tiny bit above your means, Mother dear.'

'Of course you must have realised as soon as you heard,' said Clarissa quickly, 'particularly since they had known each other before he knew you.'

Jennifer stared at her mother. She saw not just the flush of supermarket sherry, but the flush of triumph. She had seen it before when her mother had re-married. Realisation of what she was saying dawned greyly, and then twilight quickly followed, as she realised that what her mother was hinting at was all too possible. Pember had been very strange while Georgiana was staying. He had refused to stay at his fishing hotel in the manner in which a gentleman normally would, whose one idea was to escape the company of women, and in particular his wife, as soon as possible. (The only exception to this, for some reason she could never fathom, was Lady Tizzy.) And once he had returned, he had spent the whole time spying on herself and Georgiana. At the time she had imagined that it was simply and solely male jealousy, but now it seemed it might have been more, considerably more; it might have been equally simply and solely because his fascination with Georgiana had been suddenly rekindled. And Georgiana so innocent and so beguiling, throwing herself upon Jennifer's good graces when all the time she was merely an unhappy woman trying to recapture a prize she had once lost.

'It's always best friends, you know,' said Clarissa matter-of-factly. 'Every time I pick up the *Daily Mail* someone's best friend has gone off and got pregnant by *her* husband. Girls will be girls, alas, but there's nothing like—'

'Excuse me,' said Jennifer, and she put her large,

starched, linen napkin to her lips and stood up. 'Must be the mackerel.'

Her mother watched her rush from the dining room with some satisfaction, until she started to calculate the alimony that someone like Pemberton would be liable for. If it had anything to do with her, it would knock the stuffing out of even his 'Anciennes Richesses'.

The Countess was talking to her daughter, Lady Mary, on the telephone. She propped the white receiver upon her shoulder while she buttered her wholemeal toast from a Lord Roberts Workshop breakfast tray. The receiver perched quite comfortably for the duration of the spreading, and then was quickly returned to one hand, while the other posted the toast. Mary was being trying that morning. Being trying, in the Countess's book, was not committing yourself, wholeheartedly, to the Countess's point of view.

'Of course no-one knows where she is,' said the Countess, now lying back against her pillows and chewing delicately on the toast, 'and even if anyone did, I doubt whether they could make any impression upon her. However, Jennifer Pemberton is said to be going to try, but I doubt very much if she will make any headway, simply and solely because, after all, she got Pemberton right from under—'

'Not quite,' said Mary, changing her receiver from one shoulder to another so that she could continue putting nail varnish on her fingernails.

'Well,' said the Countess, 'that's how everybody read it, and when all's said and done, that's all that finally counts in the long run, isn't it?'

'I suppose so,' agreed Mary, and then bared her teeth in a sudden grimace, which was meant to be good for the complexion.

'Oh yes, that's all that matters. Of course no-one can find James. He seems to have gone to ground completely instead of having the sense to be around to clarify the situation. I suppose he'll be heartbroken, he did seem quite attached to her. I expect she's just not herself at the moment, and will soon pull herself together and go back to him. Don't you think?'

'Not really,' said Mary. 'Knowing Georgiana, she'll do nothing of the kind.'

'I hope you're wrong.'

'But you know I'm right.'

'I hope, even so, that you are wrong.'

'Oh dear, there's the bell. I must run, Mama, there's somebody coming to lunch.'

'Anyone of interest?'

'No, no-one of interest.'

They each put their telephones down. The Countess popped the last of her breakfast into her mouth and frowned. She hadn't liked Mary's tone in the least. It had been unforgiving and full of the kind of mild impatience that was not appropriate in a daughter. She pushed the tray away and rang for her girl. She had enjoyed having her breakfast at lunchtime, as she so often did; it cut the day in half and made her feel as if she was as much in demand as she had always been, in the old days.

Mary waved her hands to dry her fingernails and stopped just in time for Maria to slide into the drawing room on her Doctor Scholl sandals announcing 'Lord

167

Stranragh' in a particularly Spanish and hacienda-like way.

'James.'

'Mary.'

They both looked at each other unable to speak. Finally James said, 'I can't tell you how kind this is of you. There's no-one else—'

'No, of course not,' Mary smiled. 'Just the two of us. Like old times?'

James looked round the particularly feminine drawing room.

'It's just like old times,' he agreed.

Mary tossed her hair slightly to the side and walked over to the drinks table. Stranragh noted how elegant and cool she looked. Long legs on high heels, silk dress of subdued but impeccable taste, a cashmere cardigan draped gracefully over her shoulders.

'You're very kind,' he said again, and sat down.

Mary poured him a glass of wine.

'I want to help you any way I can.'

Stranragh looked thoughtful.

'Yes, and I think you can.'

They both smiled. And as Stranragh took the glass of wine he noted that Mary's scent was slightly too heavy, something which he would help her with, and she noted that his tie wasn't *quite* right with his shirt, something which she could help him with. And then they both smiled again.

# 8

It was Patti's favourite time of day, the time of day when she could retire to her room, lock the door, retrieve her tapestry from under the bed, and dream of Ron. It was a perfect combination of activities, spoiled only by the knowledge that she had got further with her tapestry than she had with Ron. She couldn't understand what it was exactly, but although Ron, in their few hours together every week, professed a tremendous passion for her, professing was as far as it ever got. Of course they held hands in the back row of the cinema (it had to be the cinema in case they were seen by anyone local, because as Ron said all the locals knew him, even with his helmet off). And they had what Ron called 'sessions' in her car on their way home, but that was it. He never offered to take her anywhere more intimate than the cinema, and he never did anything in the car that he would have had to arrest himself for.

If Patti had had to admit it, in court and in front of witnesses, she would have had to say that her daydreams (Elliott called them fantasies), her daydreams starring Ron and herself in the main feature, were a great deal more colourful than the reality. It was always the same, she thought; she'd dress herself up to the nines, tell the 'boys' that she was going to the cinema, rush off in a state of great excitement, meet Ron in the back row, watch the film, meet him again in the car park, drive off in another state of excitement, drive Ron home, drop him off at his Nan's, and drive home again. If she wanted that sort of relationship, she had Fulton and Elliott. But she couldn't tell Ron that, because he was quite obviously besotted about her and she didn't want to hurt his feelings.

Of course, doing tapestry did help to keep her calm, of that there was no doubt, and although she had to keep going back to the shop to see what theirs looked like, nevertheless she had managed to keep on with it without asking Elliott for help, which was a source of great pride to her, because Jennifer Pemberton had had to ring him up only last week with a problem over one of her knights on horseback. Patti's tapestry contained no knights. They held very little interest for her after having been married to a real one. Her tapestry was full of flowers and birds, and a nice big kitten in the middle, playing with a butterfly. She planned to frame it and give it to Elliott as a Christmas present, or perhaps, if things hotted up a little, to Ron's Nan for her birthday.

Over in the nursery suite, since it was Nanny's day off, Elliott was preparing Victoria for her walk. Fulton watched with interest as he changed her and put her in her best smocked top, lacy tights, and a coat with a matching bonnet, all of which had been sewn by Elliott himself.

'I don't know why Nanny never puts her in anything I've made,' sighed Elliott, 'it really is too peculiar. Every time I see Victoria being pushed out she's in something dreary that Nanny's made, or that beastly little anorak that Nanny's mother gave her. I must say I find it very irritating.'

'She prefers boys,' said Fulton, smiling at the pretty sight that Elliott now picked up to carry down to the pram. 'Nannies always do. I know mine did. She would hardly notice my sisters.'

'Don't we look the most beautiful creature?' Elliott's turn to smile at Victoria. She had her mother's looks *plus,* you could see that already. And she had that extra something that blue blood gave you, that slight hauteur in the eyes, that slight lack of chin, that special quality that nothing but proper ancestry *could* give you. Even now you could see she would make her mark on Society, and Patti's working-class origins would only prove a positive asset, like Nell Gwyn being the mother of dukes. He was very pleased with her.

'Come on, if you keep mooning over her like that we'll never get out for our walk,' said Fulton.

'Hark who's talking. Now, you bring the Laura Ashley bag with the bottled water and a change, and I'll bring a very pretty bib in case we dribble because of a tooth.'

'Very well,' said Fulton, 'but I'm not going to be done out of my turn to push today. So don't think I am.'

But Elliott had already gone, walking slowly down the back stairs to where the pram was kept. Fulton went to follow him, and then heard the rattle of the post, which was being delivered just a few hours late because the postman was a keen sportsman and only fitted posts in between his other activities (so that, if the weather was right for fishing, you were lucky to get a letter and not a five-pound trout). Not that it mattered really, for most of the post was dreary nowadays, crammed with demands of one kind or another and quite unsuitably depressing to open at any time of day, so that you

171

were quite glad when it arrived at odd times and not always at breakfast when you might not appreciate anything untoward. The art of letter writing had been quite killed by the telephone, and although he himself made occasional attempts to redress this, and refused to use Mr Bell's famous invention more than was absolutely necessary, even so it was quite apparent that it was not going to catch on again, because so few people even knew how to hold a pen any more, and even signatures were on the wane, most of them looking more like claw marks in the snow. It would not surprise him in the very least if quite soon there was a new movement back to people using seals, or personalised rubber stamps.

He leafed through a sheaf of letters all from places such as Wellingborough and Swindon, places that he imagined would be quite empty of people at night and crowded with people operating under box numbers during the day. The one exception to the depressingly anonymous correspondence was a letter, handwritten in a way that made Fulton quickly change his mind and favour the use of the telephone. It was addressed to 'Lady Patti'.

Fulton turned it over and shuddered at the *S.W.A.L.K.* scrawled across the back of the envelope. It was obviously from an ardent, and illiterate, admirer, you would not need to be Sherlock Holmes to discover that. He glanced up the stairs towards the resting Patti's bedroom and tried to calm himself. He did not expect fidelity from Patti, but neither did he expect infidelity. He didn't know quite what he expected, or what he should expect, except that deceit was not high on the list, and if this missive was what he thought it was, he was quite sure that it was not above board. He put it in his pocket. He would push the pram out with Elliott on their usual walk, and when they got to the woods he would open it and all would be revealed.

On the walk he found himself looking sadly at Victoria. That his child should have a mother who was capable of deceiving her husband was a sorry thing indeed. He didn't know how he was going to broach the subject to Elliott, but broach it he must, for good or evil, and that went for the letter as well.

Elliott finished tying the very pretty bib round Victoria and sat down on the bench beside Fulton. Fulton stared at Victoria, and then turned to Elliott.

'I am afraid something rather horrid may have happened, Ely-ot,' he said sadly. 'Something that you might not like, and I might not like.'

'That makes two of us then. No, I can't bear it. Irene hasn't overcharged for washing powder *again*?'

'No, I mean it, Ely-ot. This is sery-ot.'

'You're getting a bit camp in your old age. So? What? What? I can't bear the suspense, and I'm certainly not going to try and *guess*.'

Fulton took the letter out of his pocket and put it in Elliott's hand.

'This,' he said.

'Urgh. What a dreadful thing.'

Elliott held the envelope up by one corner in the manner of someone holding something infected.

'Now I know what people mean when they call it an "ill-formed hand". It looks as if it's been written by a sex maniac.'

'It may well have been,' said Fulton, and he retrieved

173

the letter from Elliott. 'I think, however, that it is our duty to open it for Patti, don't you?'

'Of course,' said Elliott promptly, 'but hadn't you better wait till we get home and I can steam it?'

'You make it sound like a piece of cod.'

'Which more than likely is all that it is,' said Elliott, trying to cheer him.

Fulton slit open the letter with the kind of depressed abandon of a criminal who doesn't care if he's caught. He unfolded the small closely-lined piece of blue paper and started to read. He read slowly, for the handwriting in the letter was if anything less formed than that on the envelope. He turned it over, for it continued to half-way down the other side of the paper, with various little holes, Elliott noticed, where the writer had obviously gone through the paper in his ardour of passion, or whatever it was that he had for Patti.

Fulton folded the paper and then passed it to Elliott who, while rocking the baby with one hand, held the offending sheet in the other and then turned it over on his lap, all the while continuing to rock Victoria, who smiled up at the sky and made those little noises of contentment that adults never make, probably because they never do experience such bliss.

'Well,' said Elliott, 'I don't know what we're going to do about *this*.'

'I'm glad you don't, because I don't either.'

Elliott looked at Victoria, and then swallowed. 'It's what they always say, it's the deceit that hurts, the idea that she's been going behind our backs.'

'I know, that's it, that's exactly what I thought.'

'I can't help it, I'll have to say it – I mean after all

174

we've *done* for her. I mean, quite frankly, what *haven't* we done for her?'

'Exactly, what *haven't we done*?'

'We've married her.'

'We've had her baby.'

'We've given her a roof.'

'A nanny.'

'The Duc de Berry cradle.'

'The nursery suite *completely* re-done.'

'Her own bedroom *completely* re-done.'

'Finished her knitting for her.'

'Cooked for her *every day*.'

'Bought her a new outfit for the christening, even though we didn't get ourselves anything.'

'And what's she given us?'

Their eyes turned slowly towards Victoria, who was now sleeping, head on one side, bonnet a little crooked, pink cheek resting against Elliott's favourite pram cushion (the one with the little ducks on it).

'I suppose this means divorce?' asked Elliott.

'I suppose so.' Fulton stood up, and then sat down again. 'I suppose it might mean all sorts of things.'

'I suppose you *might* get custody of Victoria,' said Elliott, trying to keep the doubt out of his voice.

'I suppose I might, but then, on the other hand, I equally might not. You know judges, they're a bit like vicars, they have funny ideas about everyone but themselves.'

'I think that if you could prove that she was going around with people who put S.W.A.L.K. on the back of their envelopes you might win custody, I think you might easily.'

'Yes, but you're not a judge. It takes sitting about in a wig and a long frock all day to achieve some of their decisions.'

'Well, I don't know. It's the *deceit* I don't like.'

'I know – the very idea of her going out and meeting S.W.A.L.K. and her not telling us.'

'Perhaps she was embarrassed?'

'I hope she was, the hussy.'

'Victoria's too good for her, you know, she really is. And I mean, it's not as if she takes the slightest interest in her. I have to drag her to the nursery in the mornings to watch Nanny bathing her, and then *only* after Madam's had her coffee. It's extraordinary. I mean, you'd think she'd take some interest.'

Elliott sighed. Fulton joined him, and then they both stared at Victoria, who by now had slid down the pram and was in a wonderfully rumpled condition.

'Even though judges wear frocks, they still think like men and, generally speaking,' said Fulton carefully, 'I think it's fair to say that they usually decide in favour of the mum because they think any mum is better than a good dad, or even two good dads and a nanny.'

'So?'

'So. Exactly. So, it seems to me, and it does honestly, that it would be best if, at this stage, we didn't stop her seeing S.W.A.L.K.'

'No, I agree,' said Elliott with a visible relief. 'I mean, face it, Patti's always had some pretty weird tastes and she's not likely to change now, is she? I mean we've weathered the Gillott crisis, I'm sure we can weather the S.W.A.L.K. affair. At least neither of them is Victoria's father, I mean at least *she's* a Melbury, and that's all that matters, don't you think?'

'Yes, but we must be *firm*, or she'll start to blackmail us. The moment she thinks she's got the upper hand, we'll have had it.'

Elliott looked from Fulton to Victoria.

'I've got news for you, she *has* got the upper hand.'

Fulton sighed. He knew Elliott was right. There was nothing they could do about Patti's behaviour and the steaming S.W.A.L.K. They could only cross their fingers and pray. At least the letter had only been full of intense, if illiterate, hero worship. Nothing crude or upsetting that might lead you to look at Patti in quite a different light. It just ranted on about how wonderful she was. It did look forward to seeing her in the cinema as usual, but that was all. Quite tame really, compared to some of the pop songs she listened to on her headphones. He sighed again.

'Time to go back?'

'Yes. I think we've made the right decision.'

Elliott straightened Victoria in her pram and then looked at Fulton.

'But what are we going to do about the letter?'

'I'll just say I opened it by mistake, but haven't read it.'

'But then she'll know we know.'

'Yes, I know, but that's no bad thing, no bad thing at all.'

'But supposing she becomes quite blatant, and says she wants S.W.A.L.K. to come and live with her at Flint House—'

'No,' said Fulton firmly, 'no, absolutely no. That's

what I mean about not being blackmailed. She can see S.W.A.L.K. whenever she wants, but she can't have a live-in S.W.A.L.K., that's absolutely not on. And if she tried to, I will rake up a few unfavourable decisions made by judges in favour of dear old dads.'

Elliott nodded. He was very grateful for Fulton's firm line on things, but it would make him feel a little better if he was quite sure that he'd stick to them, for Patti had only to start to pop a tear into her beautiful blue eyes for Fulton to crumble, and all decisions previously arrived at would be swiftly put into reverse.

'Vains I tell her we opened the letter,' said Fulton.

'Oh, very well, I'll tell her.'

Elliott took the letter and put it in his pocket.

'I've made her favourite chocolate cake for tea, so that should get us over a few hiccups.'

'Heigh ho.'

'Heigh ho indeed.'


Meanwhile, what of Georgiana? Everyone (except Fulton and Elliott) had Georgiana on their minds, one way or another, except Georgiana herself, who had only her growing girth on her mind. She felt very ill, not at all as she felt she should have done. In Italy, where she had first discovered her impregnated state, she had been prone to blame it on the change in diet, but now she just blamed 'it'. No-one had ever told her how sick a pregnant woman could be, and it was probably because if they did, she thought, as she gazed round the singularly uninspiring group of ladies who were attending the ante-natal clinic, there would never be any more births. The depressing part about pregnancy was not that you

178

got pregnant, but that other people did. No sooner had you decided that you were the first person ever to go through this unique experience than it became necessary to attend a clinic where it became all too patently obvious that pregnancy was something that could and did happen to most women – and as in the case of the woman sitting next to her, who was having her sixth, most of the time. Prior to the necessity of finding a clinic to attend (on Gus's insistence), she had thought that having a baby, although a martyrdom of sickness, was in fact a wonderful experience, because it was the result of a passionate love affair and she had read that a baby was always the logical outcome of a passionate love affair.

It was most likely that it had been Gus's delight in his own virility (something that Georgiana found a little unappealing) that had first made her feel so unique. But now that they were back in England, camping in a horrid little house with pebbledash façade and a bell that chimed, the uniqueness of it all had been left behind, somewhere under the studio bed in Italy. She had not wanted to return from Italy, but Gus had wanted his son to be born in England. They had settled on a house in South Sheen, not far from where his mother lived, because it was the only house they could possibly afford that was near both a hospital and a bus stop, which Georgiana considered essential in the circumstances. Gus had been, as usual, completely absorbed by one thing and one thing alone: a place to paint. The roof was decided upon, and he began hastily to prepare a working studio, leaving Georgiana to try and prepare a nursery.

She liked her neighbourhood for the one reason that

would never occur to Gus – she need be in no fear that her friends would see her there. She could walk to the shops in an anonymously dreadful smock bought from the local charity shop and never bother to fear being discovered. She felt as if she were a person living under cover, or who had joined some sort of secret resistance group. She enjoyed it as much as she enjoyed being with Gus and not caring any more about what people might think.

Now she was living with him permanently she discovered that Gus was very kind and completely self-absorbed, which was, in its way, restful. He didn't notice if the top button on her blouse was undone, but he would suddenly sit her down if he saw the light catching her hair in a different way and shout 'Don't move', as if she was about to be shot, and start to paint her. In short, whether he knew it or not, she saw that he worshipped her, and so she had the good manners never to take advantage of it, but left him to his routines and his old habits as much as was possible. In him she recognized the same prodigious energy that she had once found so restful in her first lover, but Gus was warm where Kaminski had been too experienced to allow that particular emotion to complicate their relationship. He was someone she had never known before. She was someone he had never known before and naturally their baby was unique, until Georgiana had to attend the maternity clinic.

'Mrs Hackett?'

Georgiana looked round the clinic from one lady to another before realising it was herself that the little Chinese lady was calling.

'Mrs Hackett?'

'Yes, of course.'

She put her small bag of knitting into her one remaining nearly worn-out Harrods bag and followed the nurse into a cubicle decorated in tasteful municipal green.

'Lie-down-there-and-roll-down-your-tights-the-doctor-will-be-with-you-in-a-minute.'

Georgiana sat down on the edge of the bed and removed her small, but now slightly worn, perfectly made shoes. (They were Italian, bought for her by Gus in a fit of passionate extravagance.)

There were still some months to go, and she knew that she was larger than was usual, but she also knew that it was better to be poor in England having a baby, than to be poor in Italy having a baby.

The curtain was flung violently aside and a man whom she took to be the gynaecologist stood glowering at her with the Chinese nurse behind.

'And whom have we got here?' he asked.

'Mrs Hackett,' said Georgiana firmly.

The gynaecologist stared down at the notes in front of him.

'Why haven't you been in before, Mrs Hackett?' he asked, as if he were a traffic warden who had found her with a wheel over a double yellow line.

'I've been in Italy.'

'I see.'

He turned towards her, and stared at her.

'On holiday?'

'No, I was living there.'

'Someone like you, I'd have thought you were holidaying.'

181

'Well, I wasn't.'

Georgiana stared up at him. He pulled her dress back almost as violently as he had flung the curtain, and placed a pair of heavy hands upon her stomach.

'You must be at least seven months,' he said, the accusation in his voice mounting.

'Yes, I am.'

'In that case why didn't you come here before?'

'Because – I was resident in Italy.'

'Someone like you,' he interrupted, 'I should have thought that you could afford the best private care in Italy. Someone like you.'

'My husband wanted the baby to be born English.'

'Next week, you'll have to come again next week.'

The Chinese nurse backed out of the cubicle to allow him to pass as Georgiana swung her legs over the side of the bed and started to pull up her stockings. She didn't understand why it was that he thought of her as 'someone like' anyone. As far as he was concerned, and as far as she was concerned now, she was Mrs Hackett. She felt like calling the whole thing off – not Gus, but the pregnancy. The enormity of what she had done now came to her, a messenger from the left, heavy-faced, with large fingers and gloomy eyes. She was down the famous cul de sac, and there was no room to escape the oncoming traffic.

She walked slowly back from the clinic, avoiding watching herself in the shop windows, her eyes trying not to see the dullness of the little shops, the uniformly stained concrete structures, the dirt that sprayed up from the roads, the people in their drab clothes. Italy had been different. In Italy there was poverty, but there was colour.

In Italy you could be poor in the morning, but by nightfall you could be rich, as, for the price of a drink, you sat out and watched the world go by with the warm air as an evening cloak.

At home she took Gus a cup of tea, 'nice and thick so that the spoon can stand up in it', and then went to the nursery and started to sew the white quilting she had bought in a linen sale on the way to attend the clinic. She was beginning to understand now what poverty was. It was having to choose between buying the quilting and having mince for supper. It was selling your little pearl and diamond brooch so that you could decorate the nursery. It was not going anywhere, because it was too expensive, and staying in with only one bar on the fire on. It was telling Gus you 'didn't feel like lunch' because he needed to eat more than you did. And yet the strange thing was, she enjoyed it. The world she had been born into had become another planet, when she considered how she could in the past have gone for months without even cooking for herself, so many and varied had been her invitations.

She missed no-one. She expected to think about them sometimes, but she didn't; living from day to day, and almost from hand to mouth, she thought only of the present hour and its demands. The fact that she was unmarried didn't trouble her any more than the fact that her husband might be looking for her. She had locked the past behind her, and for the first time in her life was experiencing the oddity of happiness. It was not something she had been brought up to consider, any more than she had ever considered unhappiness. Until Gus came back into her life, things happened to her or they didn't happen to her. She owned things or she didn't own things, but whether or not they brought her happiness was not a consideration.

Now all she had was this undemanding thing, ever present, sometimes almost tangible, called contentment. She disliked being pregnant, but she saw that it was necessary in some primitive way to Gus. She disliked the house, and she disliked the neighbourhood, but none of these things had anything to do with the fact that she was, undeniably, and for the first time in her life – happy.

Of course she never spoke to Gus about it. He spoke to her about it, and quite often, which she found, as she found everything to do with him, embarrassing, because mentioning your feelings, or even being aware of them was not what she was used to. But nothing could stop Gus discussing them, any more than anything could stop him swearing, or losing his temper, or doing any number of the one thousand things of which she could not approve. She loved everything he did, precisely because she didn't like it, and wasn't used to it; and, she came to realise, he felt exactly the same about her. There was no discord, only a perpetual fascination with each other's differences, out of which sprang a wonderful harmony.

She tried not to think about the baby as a boy or as a girl, but simply as some future event that would make life different for both of them. She knew that it wouldn't be easy, and that babies were cataclysmic disruptions to life, because she had been told they were; but, like her new-found poverty, she was determined that it would be enjoyable and that, as with the façade of her house, she would simply ignore the bits that weren't.

She knew she was not naturally maternal, but she felt sure that Gus would make up for both of them – for working-class fathers, she had heard, took a great interest in their babies, and weren't content to just visit the nursery every now and then.

And so it proved to be, for from the moment the baby arrived, it might as well have been Gus who had given birth to him. Overnight it seemed that he had lost interest in his painting and had become a fully employed father. He was hardly awake in the morning before he was in the nursery, a clean nappy flung over his shoulder, a basket of fresh laundry (done by his mother) at his elbow. If Georgiana had wanted, she could have felt jealous over his pre-occupation, but she knew her limitations, and looking after babies was one of them; and so she would lie listening to the happy sounds of baby talk and baby bath, and clouds of talcum powder would come wafting into her room as she brushed her hair, did her post-natal exercises and thought about how unexpected life could be.

Her mother-in-law was second in command in the nursery, and would arrive to push the baby out while Gus was supposedly at work – which time he used, more often than not, to have coffee with Georgiana and read the newspapers. Or, if he had been up in the night, he would fall asleep beside her on the bed and wake up only when the baby was returned.

It amused Georgiana sometimes to think of how easy her life was now, compared to when she was Lady Stranragh. She had no sense of isolation, no fear of being criticised, she was more cosseted by Gus and his mother than she had ever been by James and all their staff. And although she would sometimes catch herself looking at something in a newspaper, or a shop window, that she would like but couldn't have, the feeling would pass, and she would come back to reality with a sense of relief, which was strange, since this new reality was so lacking in the luxuries that she had always considered necessities.

She hadn't enjoyed having the baby, but Gus had made up for this by his enthusiasm. She thought all those particular realities unappealing, while he had found them riveting. Even the heavy-handed gynaecologist had succumbed to his involvement. He no longer dared to make remarks about 'people like her', but had allowed Gus to lecture him on various points of his own profession, and tactfully, in view of the fact that Gus was obviously exactly the sort of person that he thought a father should be, pretended that they were new to him.

The baby grew, strong and beautiful, and after some months he fell more and more into the care of Gus's mum, and Gus was able to go back to painting, leaving Georgiana to look after the house and its concerns, which in Georgiana's mind was, quite properly, only her concern, and which she set about transforming with all the vigour of an interior decorator hired to restore a Georgian folly.

It was a small semi-detached house, in a row of small semi-detached houses. The back gardens were long strips, the front gardens were long strips, and the houses themselves were built in such a way that all the rooms led off narrow corridors. Georgiana immediately saw potential. She drew up lists of charming ideas, features for both house and garden that would distract the eye from the long strips and the narrowness of the corridors. When Gus wasn't painting, he was being commissioned by his 'common-law wife', as he loved to call her, to paint and strip and build.

While Gus's neighbours bicycled off to their allotments dreaming of wall-to-wall carpeting, he was busy painting a *trompe l'oeil* in the hall. While they put in double glazing, he was set to work to restore plasterwork; and while they sat with tray and telly of an evening, he was on his hands and knees stencilling floorboards. And yet he never complained, even though he obviously couldn't see the necessity for it, any more than his poor mother who, while somewhat awestruck by the sudden turn of events in her son's life, was nevertheless prepared to go along with it all, so long as they assured her that they would, one day, get married.

'For the sake of the child,' she would say to Georgiana, who agreed, and yet even so prayed every night that no-one would ever find her.


Perhaps it takes knowing someone from early childhood to be able to work out their likely course of events, or perhaps it was the desperation of someone who thinks that her husband and her best friend have deceived her – whatever it was that made it possible for Jennifer alone to find Georgiana, find her she did.

She wrote to her as if nothing untoward had happened over the past six months. She told her about her own new baby ('oh dear, *another* boy, poor Pember!'), and she made it quite plain that she knew that Georgiana had been pregnant and must now have had the baby. She also asked herself to lunch.

Georgiana found the lure of seeing Jennifer, after so much had happened to her, irresistible. After all, life finally becomes very dull if there is no-one to discuss its excitements with, and if there was one subject that she couldn't discuss with either Gus or his mother, it was the fact that Lady Georgiana Stranragh, formerly Longborough, had run off with a painter. From their point of view, it wouldn't be tactful. So what she had done, and why she had done it, remained unanswered to the world, or more importantly, to her world. The urge for confession was too much. She wrote back to Jennifer asking her to lunch.

Naturally there were some preparations to be made. She couldn't do anything about South Sheen, but she could make sure they were alone, because tolerant as he might be of her, Georgiana knew without having to ask him that Gus would not understand someone like Jennifer. So, when she answered her chiming doorbell to a determinedly calm Jennifer, Georgiana had the house to herself.

Jennifer's smile was sort of set about her lipstick in a wavering line, and she stepped too quickly into Georgiana's little hall, as if she couldn't wait for someone to shut South Sheen out.

'My dear, don't you look *well*.'

Georgiana smiled. Jennifer was a person from another world in this small suburban house, whereas she, she suspected, was beginning to look part of it.

'But how *charming*.'

Jennifer looked round the palely painted hall with its

188

*trompe l'oeil* of trees and flowers and its decorated floorboards. They could have been in a little folly on someone's large estate, and she only wished they were, for seeing Georgiana in a place like this was pathetic. 'I know exactly what you mean,' said Pemberton when she tried to explain at dinner that night, 'just like when you see a thoroughbred in a riding school, breaks your heart.'

'Brought you a little something,' said Jennifer, and she thrust a basket at Georgiana.

'How sweet of you.'

Georgiana looked under the cloth.

'Thought you might not get country things out – here. So I brought you one of our own chickens, and some organic veggies and things.'

'A food parcel.'

Jennifer followed Georgiana into the sitting room. (No-one could describe it, not even in their wildest dreams, as a drawing room.)

'Oh, but how dear. The bare look, so sensible.' ('Not a *thing* to sit on,' she told Pember later, 'just that sort of furniture you see in grooms' flats with patchwork quilts thrown over. Pathetic. I mean, after all she had and all she was. Too pathetic for words.')

'So.'

'So.'

The two girls smiled at each other, and Jennifer noted with slight annoyance that Georgiana's figure was as perfect as ever, in spite of having had a baby. In fact, if you didn't know how reduced she must be, you would have to admit, in spite of everything, that she did look stunning; but then that's what made it all so pathetic, really, that someone like her should *choose* to live in such a way. It was incomprehensible.

'Would you like a glass of wine?'

'If you're sure—'

Georgiana brought back a tray from the kitchen. It proudly displayed a bottle of cold white wine, bought from saving up all Gus's empty beer bottles. She felt sorry for Jennifer, because she was obviously finding it all so embarrassing, and at the same time she couldn't help finding it funny. Jennifer had such black lines under her eyes, and was so visibly nervous and strained, she must have been living in a state of dread for weeks. It was as if Georgiana had been involved in a traffic accident and done something terrible to herself, something dreadfully disfiguring, for Jennifer could hardly look her in the face.

'Where's the baby?' Jennifer asked brightly, after a short silence.

'Out with his Nan.'

'Oh, so you have got a nanny, after all?'

'After all what?'

'Well, you know, after *all*.'

'It's Gus's mum,' said Georgiana. 'She does everything for him, which is lovely.'

'Heavens, how – fortunate.'

'Yes, she's a mum in a million,' agreed Georgiana.

Jennifer leant forward.

'Do you want to talk about it?' she asked.

Georgiana's large expressive eyes stared into Jennifer's small anxious ones. It would, now that she was actually faced with it, be very difficult for her to explain anything to Jennifer. Not only that, but she had the feeling that it might be . . . distasteful. Sympathetic as Jennifer had been to Georgiana's difficulties and her unhappiness with Stranragh, she was not suddenly going to find her sympathetic to someone such as Augustus Hackett Esq. To try and explain passion to someone else would be pretty asinine.

'Shall we have lunch?'

'Just a boiled egg, I hope?'

'No, not boiled – *à la crème*.'

They ate in a stilted way, as if they were both all too aware that Georgiana had had to go to too much trouble to produce this meal. If they had been lunching in Knightsbridge in Jennifer's house, they would no doubt have just had a glass of wine and a sandwich in a relaxed way in the 'drawing room', but because of Georgiana's straitened circumstances, they sat down to lunch with small starched napkins and flowers and a cloth that Gus's mum had found in the back of her linen cupboard, which was normally only brought out for Christmas, sparkling wine glasses, and forks that shone with the effort of polishing but tasted funny when you put them in your mouth. ('Pathetic, all so pathetic.')

Now that Georgiana had made up her mind not to talk about Gus to Jennifer, they could only talk about Stranragh, and that was, largely, really rather old territory. Jennifer's attitude to Stranragh was somewhat impatient. She kept referring to him as a 'nuisance', as if he were a dog that couldn't be trusted too near other people's furniture.

Of course, although she didn't say so, she didn't believe that Stranragh had really had evil designs on Georgiana, because such melodramatic intents did not appeal to her pragmatic nature. In her mind men could (and should) always be 'managed', and it seemed to her even now that, had Georgiana only behaved a little more reasonably, she could have obtained a nice divorce in her favour that would have left her well off, comfortable, and in possession of a great deal more than she was at present. But, as she knew only too well, Georgiana was hot-blooded and impetuous, although just how impetuous and hot-blooded, she had yet to find out.

'Coffee?'

'If you're sure—'

The kettle, placed upon the gas stove, took ages to boil, so that it meant that Jennifer had ample time to 'take in' Gus's pictures. And ghastly things they were too, she thought. Dreadfulnesses that didn't look like anything that you could put your finger on. Splodges and blobs and things; things that you could never hang anywhere, or near anything. Whatever else she had or had not done, Georgiana had obviously not run off with Rembrandt.

'Mmm, what wonderful coffee. Do you think I could have another cup?'

She had whiled away a great deal of time now, talking about everything under the sun, and yet still the wretched baby was not back with his nanny, or his grandmother, or whatever she was.

Georgiana collected Jennifer's cup and hoped she would go soon, for she had promised Gus that he could return for tea, and it seemed that Jennifer would never go, and that she would still be in residence when he returned, which would never do.

'Oh look, here's Nan and the baby.'

Jennifer's cup rattled loudly as she replaced it on its saucer.

'Oh look, so it is,' she said, as a homely-looking person, in a tidy kind of macintosh, pushed a beautiful blonde baby into the small hall.

Georgiana picked the baby out of its pram and turned it towards Jennifer, whose *smile fixe* was becoming rapidly unpeeled.

'Isn't he beautiful?'

Georgiana looked down at him proudly, as Jennifer stared fiercely into his face searching for any traces of Pember.

'He's a Hackett from the top of his head to the tips of his toes,' said the baby's Nan proudly. 'Look, he's even got Gus's funny fingers and those funny square nails of his. As I said to Georgie here, if he gives you any trouble, pet, he can't give you no trouble about who the father of his child is, and that's for sure. Not a bit. It's Augustus all over again, more's the pity; but I could show you pictures of him, as a baby, and you couldn't tell a twin of difference.'

Now Jennifer was pinching the baby's cheek in an immediately fond way, and then she was kissing Georgiana goodbye, more lovingly than she could ever have imagined kissing any member of her own sex. She would come to see her again soon. It had all been such fun. Really. Such fun. And she must bring Gus and the baby down to Wiltshire, of course. Wonderful to see her so settled and happy, at last.

She ran down the little suburban road to where her Porsche was parked discreetly outside someone else's house, and felt so happy that she didn't even mind when she realized that some horrid little toad had run their front door key all down the side of it.

# 9

The Countess looked round her new drawing room, a last-minute check to make sure that everything was looking as it should. Fulton and Elliott were coming to tea. She was looking forward to it, but she was in slight dread that they might find something to comment about, particularly since she had 'saved' on using a decorator. Perhaps it was moving to Wiltshire after the increasing suburbia of Sussex, but the slightest lapse would, she knew, be apparent, and being apparent would be observed by one of them.

They arrived punctually, which was always pleasing, and they looked pleasant, which was doubly pleasing. 'Tea' was an increasing custom in the country, she found, because everyone was so busy trying to save. Hers was to be a magnificent affair. Tiny scones, with fresh cream and home-made jam from the delicatessen, triangles of toast with gentlemen's relish, and a special sort of chocolate cake.

'Well.'

'Well.'

They all looked round the room and the Countess could tell straightaway that they liked it, because they said nothing at all, as people always do when something is right.

'I've gone for the faded look,' she said.

'It suits you,' said Elliott

'Perfectly,' said Fulton.

Just for a second she was happy, because although she knew she had impeccable taste, there was nevertheless a tiny bit of her that liked it to be confirmed. But then, quickly following this feeling came another one of unease. It happened seldom or never that Fulton and Elliott both liked something, both at the same time, and so she knew immediately that they must be going to try and sell her one of their horrid bits of 'cannibalized' mock furniture.

'I've banished the ancestors to the halls and corridors, even the "stunner", because I'm fed up with people telling me I look like them,' she said. 'I was beginning to *feel* like them.'

They went in to tea in the dining room.

'You see I haven't even hung any in here.'

'Perfection,' said Fulton gravely, which caused the Countess's eyes to travel, in some desperation, to every corner of the room, making sure that there were no empty spaces where they could suggest putting one of their reproductions.

'So.'

'So,' said Elliott, his mouth full of scone and cream.

'How's life at Flint House?' asked the Countess, hoping that they wouldn't mention the baby.

'Pretty perfect,' said Fulton.

'Really? How dull. I always think perfection is too *even*, like no laughter in heaven.'

'Victoria Eugenia,' said Elliott, his mouth full once more, 'is so beautiful.'

'Of course she is, all babies are beautiful, that is their

tragedy,' said the Countess quickly. 'Do you think she'll be plain or coloured?'

Elliott so far forgot himself that he nearly said, 'Neither, she doesn't have to be, she's a Melbury.'

'She's going to be a stunner,' said Fulton, with quiet certainty.

'I'm afraid I find other people's babies even more boring than my own.'

'I used to,' said Fulton, 'but now,' he sighed, 'now I can think of nothing else. You know how it is, it's the way things go. Remember when we all had a craze for jigsaws? Remember? And everywhere we went, every view we saw, we kept making into jigsaws?'

'Of course I remember,' said Elliott with feeling. 'I couldn't look at a wall without wondering how many pieces it would break into. And as for a blue sky and clouds, or a gravelled drive, they became torture.'

'That's how it is with babies, I find,' said Fulton to the Countess, who was so bored she was cutting the chocolate cake, even though they weren't 'on' the toast yet. 'I can't pass someone else's pram without peering into it to see if theirs is better than ours. I lie awake at night wondering if she's still breathing. I no longer take any interest in anything in Harrods except the baby department, and spend fortunes on her clothes while I myself am in rags. It's pathetic.'

'It's because you're a late father,' said the Countess. 'It always hits them worse.'

'We're both late fathers,' agreed Elliott, which Fulton found quite touching, because it was the first time he had ever publicly admitted to being even the same generation as Fulton.

197

The Countess twitched her napkin over her knee, dismissing an imaginary fly from somewhere. She did not want to talk about babies. She wanted everyone to be in a pretty, cleverish sort of mood, in a world where everyone remained exactly as they were when they were sitting in their baths dreaming; stylish, witty, and surprisingly wise.

'I've thought of my "last words",' she said, pushing the chocolate cake away from her.

Fulton and Elliott waited.

'There are very few things in life that cannot be improved by chopped parsley.'

'Very good,' said Fulton quite seriously.

'Will you want it scattered on the coffin?'

'Definitely,' the Countess asserted. 'How about you?'

'Oh, I think Ely-ot will need crushed garlic.'

They all laughed, and the Countess knew she had 'drawn them off' babies.

'You know, I think I'm getting to feel a little dulled, now I've finished the house.'

'People always do. That's the moment you either feel like moving again, or you give a party.'

'I don't want to do either.'

'You could buy a horse.'

'Or take up flying.'

'Quite, or I could put in for becoming a JP, but I'm not in the mood, you know.'

'Of course,' said Elliott, eyeing the chocolate cake but feeling too shy to ask for a piece.

'Why not give a party somewhere else, a different sort of party, you know?'

'What, you mean a masked ball in a Roman Bath, or something. I don't think so.'

'No, something really different—'

'How about giving a Tesco Party? No-one's done that.'

'How would it go?'

'Well,' said Elliott, pulling the chocolate cake towards him, 'everyone could dress up as really dreary customers, and you could give it on a Sunday, and they could bring all their screaming children, and there would be a prize for the most repulsive family.'

He popped the chocolate cake dexterously on to his plate as the other two laughed.

'That does sound fun.'

'You would certainly make your mark in Wiltshire with that,' said Fulton.

'It's not that I want to make my mark, it's just that I hate feeling dulled, you know?'

They both nodded, because they knew exactly what she meant. It was how they had felt before Victoria Eugenia arrived in their lives and demanded their attention twenty-four hours a day.

'I thought of getting a telescope and studying the night sky, but it's such a cold occupation, and I'm not sure I want to see a flying saucer anyway, or meet a man from Mars, not at my age, I don't think we'd have much common ground.'

'Why,' said Elliott, his mouth full of the lovely fluffy chocolate cake, 'why don't you go into business again with Andrew?'

'Andrew's got to go to China with a party of dowagers, or else Mrs Gillott is going to cut him out of her will.'

'Still, I suppose he will come back?'

'Not if Mrs Gillott has anything to do with it.'

'It's going that well, is it?'

The Countess didn't reply. She didn't like to think back to the day she had had tea with Mrs Gillott, it reminded her too sombrely of her niece, and her folly. It was now, of course, because it wasn't amusing, a forbidden subject as far as she was concerned, although she was quite sure that this would not be so for Fulton and Elliott, who, she felt certain, would have spoken of nothing else for the past few months. She hated scandals to do with her family, and now it seemed she had to be resigned to the fact that Georgiana was one of those people who trailed chaos in her wake. It had even been mentioned in the paper last week under the heading, 'Lady Georgie Bolts Again'. They were calling her the New Bolter, and the wretched Stranragh was suing for the return of his child, which it had been less than gently hinted was not his child at all. Where they found the people to spill all these beans, heaven alone knew – for Stranragh still hadn't found her.

'Of course everyone is in business nowadays, aren't they?' she said, suddenly returning to the subject in hand.

'People even pretend to be when they're not. Business and meanness is all the rage.'

'I suppose I could do something with Americans, you know, like Lavinia does. Wear my tiara and have tea with them, things like that.'

'Admirable. And then there's the garden. In the summer you could open it on behalf of the National Gardens Scheme, particularly if you're going to make a water garden, as you said the other day.'

'Yes, that *would* be fun.'

The Countess smiled over towards the garden.

'I'll have to get someone to help me, because I'm not very good with bog flowers, or whatever you need.'

'And the field, you'll have to turn it into a wild flower garden to encourage butterflies.'

'Yes, wild flowers and butterflies have always gone together wonderfully, haven't they?'

This was a charming allusion which Fulton and Elliott appreciated. The Countess stood up. She felt like a glass of champagne. She rang for Mrs Eason. The 'boys' had made her feel much better. They had knocked the edges off her dullness, and she could even face having Andrew over for dinner now, which since his 'stay' with her when she was moving in had been unheard of. She had never thought that she would feel any sympathy for Mrs Gillott, but after putting up with Andrew for four horrendous weeks, she had felt she could almost *like* the woman, if only because she kept the wretch out of everyone's else's way.

His 'help' had consisted of drinking all her cellar, dropping all her china, and causing the builder deep offence by constantly referring to him, directly, as 'that silly little man'. And then he had persisted in going to the neighbouring village all the time, a habit which had annoyed her so much that she had followed him one day, on the pretence that she had forgotten to remind him to get some cream crackers. She had found him parked outside the village shop gossiping with Lady Tizzy and ogling her in the most revolting way as if she was the last woman on earth. That had been a very black mark indeed, and their already strained relationship had been strained even further by his getting drunk and confessing that he had always loved Patti with a passion known only to the desperately unattractive middle-aged man.

'This is just nature copying art,' the Countess had kept muttering, remembering the *canard* she had put around about Andrew being the father of Lady Tizzy's baby.

Putting him to bed had been frightful. He so heavy and she increasingly frail from the wretched arthritis. He had insisted on going to bed in his clothes, which she had finally had to yield to, even though the sheets were quite fresh and new, and the thought of him lying in them in his smoky clothes kept her awake half the night.

She smiled at Fulton and Elliott as they took their leave after helping her out with the champagne. They had made her feel *much* better, as they no doubt knew. They were very kind to her, and she did appreciate it just now, when she seemed to have landed herself in a bit of a backwater. There was plenty to which to look forward. Having Americans to tea, which should be hilarious. Making the water garden. Planting wild flowers to encourage butterflies. The future seemed roseate, and not at all dull.

Elliott kissed her fondly. Fulton paused before following suit.

'You know, I was just thinking,' he said, 'I was just thinking about how beautiful you've made everything.'

The Countess smiled.

'And then I was just remembering a dear little piece that would be perfect just here.'

The Countess continued to smile; there was nothing else she could do in the circumstances.

'Yes?'

'Yes. I think I'll bring it round in the morning, and you can try it out. I think you'll be pleased.'

'I'm sure I shall,' said the Countess, and closed the door with a little sigh.

Patti had returned to Flint House ahead of Fulton and Elliott. She hated the house when they were out. It seemed so dark and lonely, and it brought back memories of dear Knightey, whom she had been remembering most fondly in contrast to the wretched Ron. Knightey had been devoted and untiring in his appreciation of her, she realised now. He had been passionate in a wonderful way that Ron most definitely wasn't. He had been fun too, in his own sweet way. Always up to something like getting drunk, or taking her out to dinner, always full of some new idea – not at all like Ron, who, she thought with increasing anger, was quite happy for her to pay not only for the cinema seats, but also the wamburgers and the double zings. Honestly, the more she thought about it, the more angry she got, and as if that wasn't the double biscuit, now, tonight, he had had the gall to call the whole thing off himself, as if, would you credit it, as if he had been financing it.

She went up to her bedroom, shut the door and locked it. She sat down at her ruched and netted dressing table and stared hard at herself. She was still on the young side. Her body was still beautiful, she had good statistics, as good as any in the paper, and where was it getting her, absolutely nowhere. Nowhere, but nowhere, and fast. She picked up a piece of hair and sprayed it viciously. Never in her whole life had she been finished with. Not ever. And now it had happened. It was the beginning of the end. She knew how great actresses felt in their decline. Alone and vulnerable, with only things like tapestry to take their minds off the sinking sensation. And not even tapestry was all that it was cracked up to be, because even that was fraught with difficulties no one warned you about. She picked up her small frame and threw it under the bed. It had all gone wrong, and there was no getting away from it.

She sat down once more in front of her mirror. The trouble with her life was that she was not doing the one thing she was really good at. The one thing for which she had been brought up. She was not realizing her potential, and what was worse, nor was anyone else.

The doorbell rang. Patti went and stood by her own door, and listened. It couldn't be Fulton and Elliott because they were out, and anyway they lived here, and had doorkeys. It couldn't be Nanny, because she was in the wing watching television. The only person it could be was someone she hadn't thought of. She unlocked the bedroom door very quickly, and pulled her skirt down. She'd be able to see who it was through the glass top of the front door and if whoever they were wasn't the person she was hoping (i.e. Ron come back with an apology, and an offer of a fresh start), then she could shut the shutters very quickly and her skirt could do whatever it wanted.

She walked carefully downstairs on her very high stiletto heels, and then faced the front door. The outside light was on and she could see quite clearly who it was. She pulled her skirt down even further. She knew he'd come back to her. He couldn't resist it, she thought, the colour coming into her cheeks with excitement. Mind you, she must remember to keep cool, and not show how pleased she was.

'Come in, quick, before Nanny sees. She's in the wing.'

She pulled the shutters over and stood facing him. A magnificent sight, her front wobbling with great certainty, her legs, always one of her best features, encased in their seamed stockings, an even more magnificent sight. Pemberton gazed at her, his ardour having reached uncontrollable heights. It was a close run thing with Patti, which her best feature really was, and just at that moment he didn't really care.

'Lady Tizzy—'

'We haven't got much time,' said Patti suddenly, hearing the grandfather clock on the landing striking.

'Lady Tizzy—'

'Where do you want to go?'

'Well.'

'You know, my place or yours?'

This was fast even for Pemberton.

'I've really missed you, you know, Lady Tizzy, all these months. I expect you thought I was an absolute—'

'See, Fulton and Elliott will be back in a minute, and it doesn't give us long.'

Pemberton was determined to continue with his prepared speech.

'And what's more, I know how wonderful you've been about the—'

Patti stamped her foot.

'Quick, they'll be back any minute.'

Pemberton abandoned his attempted speech.

'I've left my car by the gate,' he said, 'and Jennifer's in London.'

Patti gave out a small whoop of pleasure.

'Great. I'll leave a note for the boys, and tell them not to expect me back till late, and off we go.'

She turned and opened the front door. Pemberton's eyes fixed themselves on her stocking seams. He knew they were stockings, he just knew it, because Patti, unlike Jennifer, disdained tights. Ghastly things that made the bottom half of a woman look like a bank robber. His knees buckled slightly as he followed her down the short carriage drive. An evening such as this he had not bargained for; all he had hoped for was a sort of glimpse of the former delights he had once enjoyed. Now here he was, Jennifer-less and with an empty house.

'What's that you've got in your hand?' asked Patti as she sidled into his car, her leather skirt creaking slightly.

'RSPCA box. Jennifer's RSPCA box. I was coming round for a collection.'

Patti grinned.

'Well, you've collected then, haven't you?'

'Yes, I have.'

Pemberton drew closer to her.

'You know you're a woman in a million, don't you?'

Patti nodded.

'I sure do.'

Pemberton put out his hand, but Patti pushed it away.

'Don't be silly, not now JP. Wait till we get up to the house.'

Pemberton smiled.

'Wise, warm and wonderful,' he sighed happily.

They parked the car and crept in the side door of

the Hall, because Patti was afraid that Bloss might see her.

'You can trust Bloss, you know,' said Pemberton, 'really, I even trust him with my port.'

'You can't tell on port,' said Patti. 'You can tell on Patti.'

'I'll have to tell him I won't be down for dinner,' said Pemberton.

'All right. Tell him to send it up, but you'll come out and fetch it.'

'No, I don't think he'd like that, that would be a break in his routine,' said Pemberton, frowning.

'Oh come on, either you want to, or you don't.'

'No,' said Pemberton, finishing off his train of thought, 'I know what I will do. I'll tell him to bring the tray to the bottom of the stairs, and then I'll take it up myself. Oh, and I'd better remind him to lay for two.'

'But if you tell him to lay for two, he'll know there's two of us up there,' said Patti, starting to laugh.

'Yes, but he won't know it's you, so it won't matter, will it?'

Patti was already at the top of the back stairs.

'Tell him what you like,' she whispered. 'I'll be waiting for you.'

Just for a minute Pemberton felt almost dizzy. It was sheer bliss on wheels, the whole thing. The best things in life happened spontaneously and naturally, he had always maintained, and there was no doubt about it, Patti was certainly natural and, if his memory served him right, pretty spontaneous. He watched her disappearing out of sight with deep appreciation, and then he turned to go and find Bloss.

'Oh, Bloss, there you are,' he said. 'You're always where I least expect you.'

Bloss emerged from the shadows, and smiled.

'Anything wrong, m'lord?' he asked.

'Wrong. Far from it,' said Pemberton, smiling. 'It feels as Christmas should, and never does.'

'One of your lordship's usuals in the pantry?'

'Yes, but I can't take too long about it. I've a – I'm entertaining a friend tonight, Bloss. A friend who wishes to remain anonymous, for reasons I can't disclose. We would like dinner for two, consequently, brought to the bottom of the stairs to avoid embarrassment and confusion. You know the sort of thing.'

'Of course, sir,' said Bloss pouring his lordship's usual, plus. 'Will the friend be staying all night, m'lord?'

'No,' said Pemberton, 'I regret to say not, but you needn't concern yourself about that, just leave all that to me.'

Bloss poured himself his usual, plus.

'Cheers, m'lord.'

'Absolutely, Bloss. Double cheers, triple cheers, in fact.'

'I hope you have a good evening.'

'I will, Bloss. I will, don't you worry.'

Bloss watched him disappearing out of the pantry door. This was the first time for many months that his lordship had not lingered for a gossip and a chat, but speaking for himself he was not put out by this. His lordship had not been having much fun lately. His lordship had been one could almost say persecuted by her ladyship, and for no reason that either he, or his lordship, could fathom. She had only to see him coming in through one door, for her to disappear out another. And try as they both had to find out the reason for her antipathy, they had, unquestionably, failed, he thought, no question of that. It was a strange thing that a handsome rich man, such as his lordship undoubtedly was, should put up with such behaviour from his wife, who was, when all was said and done, a plainish sort of person, without a single drop of noble blood in her own veins. But then his lordship had been in poor shape when he met her. He had been recovering from a long affair with Poppy Sydmouth, who was the sort of girl who used to send down for peanut-butter sandwiches at two o'clock in the morning and throw all his lordship's underclothes out of his dressing room window. Not the sort of girl staff would stay for, and most of them had left during that era, all except for himself, who was able to put up with her only because he had faith in his lordship finally tiring of her, which he did indeed do. But then, naturally, he had to replace that box of fireworks with something quite different, and so one way or another, he had found her ladyship and married her on the rebound, and she had given him boy after boy, and there was no doubt he was grateful for them, and so willing to put up with a certain amount of what his lordship called 'mareishness', only just lately it had developed into something more like 'bitchiness'.

It had been making his lordship most unhappy. He had complained that his hair was falling out (and indeed Bloss had found more than was usual in his ivory brushes) and that he found difficulty in completing *The Times* crossword in the morning. All bad signs for a man who had the normal calm nature of someone who has been born into a great title and enormous wealth. Although, of course, Bloss knew, and no-one better, that neither of these things protected you from the normality of life. 'You can only sleep in one bed at a time,' his old mother used to say, and how true it was.

Bloss prepared the perfect supper for a gentleman entertaining the lady of his choice. Champagne, of course, quail's eggs with special salt, and one of Mrs Bilston's special chicken pies accompanied by small parsley potatoes and petit pois. He couldn't find a nice little silver dish into which to put the petit pois, so he improvised with a muffin dish.

He stood back to take it all in. And a very pretty sight it all presented. He glanced at the old schoolroom clock that now dominated the kitchen. It was exactly half past eight.

Pemberton padded happily down to the foot of the stairs. There was Bloss all ready and waiting, and with exactly the sort of supper that a chap and his lady fancied.

'I say, Bloss, this looks splendid.'

'Just a little something, m'lord.'

Pemberton took the tray, and Bloss watched him climbing the stairs. He had wanted to say 'just a little something for your little something', but had thought that would be going too far.

'I say, m'lord, just leave the tray outside the door. I'll attend to the rest.'

'You're a wonderful chap, Bloss,' said Pemberton.

'Yes, I am, aren't I?' said Bloss to himself. 'Even though I say it who shouldn't.'

And he poured himself another double, and switched on the telly.

'Oh not those horrible rubbery quails eggs, I hate those,' said Patti.

'Have some Melba toast instead—'

'Elliott always has those, and I hate them.'

'Chicken pie, potatoes and peas?'

'That's more like it.'

Patti kissed the top of Pemberton's head.

'You know something? I really love you, you know that?'

Just for a second Pemberton felt worried. He couldn't really tell Patti that he didn't want her to love him, not the way people loved each other who got married and divorced a great deal, anyway.

Patti pinched his cheek.

'Not like that, silly,' she said. 'You don't have to worry, I won't make any trouble for you. No, I love you because you appreciate me. You appreciate what I am, and I like that, I can't say that I don't.'

'I think you're wonderful,' said Pemberton with great sincerity. 'Quite wonderful.'

'Do you? Well that's very sweet of you, JP. No, really.' Patti removed the pastry from her chicken and peered underneath it to see what it was hiding. It didn't look too mucked about, so she cut carefully into it.

Pemberton raised his champagne glass to her.

'To my Lady Tizzy,' he said, adding, 'don't drink to yourself, it's unlucky.'

She was just as beautiful as ever, sitting in one of his father's old Sulka dressing gowns, all tousled and tumbled, and gloriously stacked. She restored his faith in girls and their sweetness. She had never made any attempts to pin her pregnancy on him, nor had she asked for money, or made any vulgar references to the baby at all. It was as if it had never happened, which made him doubly proud of her and the baby. Of course, when it grew up a little, he would naturally 'help' the child, as only a really rich godfather could. He would not stand by and see her struggling to find money to educate her, and that sort of thing. She must, as a Melbury by-blow, have everything that was fitting, but it would all be handled discreetly, and a large part of this 'discretion' was due to Lady Tizzy's tact.

She leant against him, putting out her glass for more champagne.

'You know I'll have to get back to the boys soon, don't you?'

'Certainly I do,' said Pemberton, 'but not before—'

'No, no, of course not, but just in case you think I've got more time than I have. OK?'

Pemberton started to eat more quickly. Every minute of Lady Tizzy's time was precious to him. Suddenly the short two miles between the Hall and Flint House seemed to be a vast unending prairie. He wished they could be together always, but knew it would never be possible, and consequently the next two hours were quite rapturous, in a way that, he realized afterwards, they could never be if Lady Tizzy was able to stay.

Bloss awoke, as he always did, to the sound of the television signal, loud and clear. He switched it off and then glanced at his watch. He had forgotten to 'clear' the tray, but it didn't matter as he was quite sure that his lordship was now fast asleep. He walked into the silent hall, and was about to switch on the light when it became illuminated by the unmistakeable lights of her ladyship's car. He quickly froze, and then equally quickly unfroze and started to leap up the stairs to his lordship's rooms with all the agility of a man who sees his comfortable life about to pass in front of his eyes.

The tray was not in place. He pushed the door open. His lordship was lying asleep upon the bed in an abandoned state, as was Lady Tizzy. The room was littered. In every corner there was something untoward. He was suddenly glad he'd done National Service.

'M'lord, quick. Lady Tizzy, it's her ladyship.'

As he let fly these emotive words he set about the room, collecting everything in a random way, so that intimate items and glasses and food were all cleared into the nearest receptacle, which happened to be the linen basket.

'Hang on,' said Patti, starting to laugh. 'You've put my bra in the pie dish.'

'Never mind that,' said Pemberton, removing a crust. 'Just get out of here.'

Bloss staggered down the corridor bearing the linen basket in one hand and pulling the still-laughing Patti after him.

'Good job I parked round the back, eh, Bloss?' said Patti, as she flung the greater part of her clothes into the back seat.

'Put her in gear, Lady Tizzy, and I'll push,' said Bloss in a low voice.

'I've got a feeling you've done this before,' said Patti.

'Never mind that,' said Bloss. 'Just pray his lordship remembers to put his pyjamas on.'

It had taken Jennifer an age to get into the house, due to the burglar alarm, and Bloss not being up, and one thing and another, but now that she was, she stood contentedly in the hall looking with real affection at her reproduction bronze African shield and the new suit of armour that Elliott had had made for her to stand by the walking sticks. It was really lovely to be home, more lovely than it had ever been. She had been going to stay in London, after lunching with Georgiana, but somehow she had found it too lonely without Pember. Her dear Pember, whom she had so badly mistaken for the sort of person he could never be. So here she was all ready to surprise him. She hoped and prayed that he would still be awake, and that they would be able to sit and have one of their little 'cosies' together, as they used to do.

Certainly his light was still on, because she saw that when she drove up, so he might, with luck, still be reading.

'Pember?'

'Mmm?'

'Pember, darling, it's me, Jennifer.'

'Who?'

'No not who, sweetie, Jennifer.'

'Oh yes, come in. I thought you were in London.'

Jennifer stood in the doorway.

'Well, I'm not.'

'So I see.'

'Is that all you have to say?'

'No, but it'll do for now.'

'There's a funny smell in here.'

'Is there?'

'Yes, it smells of food, and things.'

'Did you come all the way from London to tell me that?'

'No. I came all the way from London to surprise you.'

'Well I am.'

'What?'

'Surprised.'

Jennifer sat down on Pemberton's bed. He sat up and looked at her. It would be useless to remind Jennifer of the old and, in his opinion, very wise adage 'never surprise a man or a dog', because even if she knew it, she would not, quite obviously, agree with it.

'Pember.'

Jennifer looked at him. He looked so sweet and charming, and she felt so terrible about being horrid to him, now that she knew that she had had no reason to be so.

'Pember.'

*'Yes.'*

'Don't get cross.'

'Why not?'

'Because it's – horrid.'

'Very well.'

'And anyway, you've got your pyjamas on the wrong way round.'

Jennifer started to laugh.

'Oh, Pember, you look so silly. Quick, get out of bed and I'll straighten you out.'

'No. I like them like this, they're – lucky.'

'Very well, then I'll get into bed and straighten them for you.'

'No, no, I tell you I like them like this.'

215

But it was far too late. Jennifer was now undressing. Pemberton closed his eyes, blocking out the sight of her tights. It was all such a hideous contrast to the earlier part of the evening.

'I'm feeling very loving,' Jennifer informed him as she crawled into bed beside him and started to undo his pyjamas. 'Isn't that nice?'

'No.'

Jennifer laughed.

'Not in a very passionate mood? That's not like my Pember.'

Her Pember groaned, but for his sins, his ladyship refused to be put off.


'Bloss,' said Pemberton thoughtfully the next evening when they were having their 'usual' in the pantry.

'Yes, m'lord?'

'I was thinking.'

'Yes, m'lord?'

'That Robin Reliant of yours. It doesn't look quite as substantial as I would like.'

'Really, m'lord?'

'No, it doesn't. I'd like to think of you driving around in something more solid. You're very valuable to me, you know, Bloss, and everyone drives so fast in the country, I'd like to think of you having more in front of you.'

'That's very kind of you, m'lord.'

'No, not kind, just realistic. How about an estate car of some kind? Of your choice. A new one, of course.'

'That would be very nice, m'lord.'

'Good, well that's settled then.'

'Only one thing though, won't her ladyship object? She put in for one for Nanny if you remember, and you came up with a Mini, which Nanny hasn't found as satisfactory as she had hoped.'

'Never mind that, Bloss, leave all that to me. You're a great deal more important than Nanny.'

Bloss smiled.

'Cheers, m'lord.'

'Cheers, Bloss.'

# 10

Georgiana had at last been tracked down by Stranragh, and was being besieged by lawyers' letters that were crammed with names on their letter heading. So many names thought Georgiana, it made you dizzy to read them. Stranragh wanted what he thought was his son back. It was stupid of him to imagine that he was so virile that he could make a baby in one go, but that, it seemed, was what he did. It would all be solved by blood tests and things, as everything was nowadays, but until it was, she lived in dread of the baby being snatched by James and taken to Italy, or somewhere. As a result of this she had sent him to stay permanently with his Nan, where he was now indistinguishable from the rest of the children being pushed out to the shops in their blue nylon anoraks and their Swiss-style nylon wool mittens.

She missed him, but not as Gus missed him. He missed him with a deep maternal longing that was touching. One good consequence of this was that he was forced to work harder than he would normally have done. One bad consequence of this was that he produced very morbid abstracts which were, to Georgiana's mind, quite unsaleable. People, she felt, who wanted to buy pictures, would not want to buy Gus's for they would make them feel very depressed, and it seemed silly for them to buy pictures that would make them feel worse about life. It just wouldn't make sense.

There was very little use in her pretending to understand Gus's work, any more than she understood him, but she did understand that they were not solvent.

She often thought of ringing former friends and acquaintances, and asking them round to see if they would like to buy any of his paintings, but each time she faced her former address book her courage evaporated. It would sound like begging, she realised, and she couldn't beg for herself and begging for Gus would be unforgivable, making him seem less in both their eyes. For the first time in her life she regretted that she wasn't clever, or even just talented. It would be so useful to be either one, or the other. She knew people who were, of course, people who had transformed equally bad circumstances by discovering they could do something that was either useful or decorative. She had only ever concentrated on being decorative herself, and now she had discovered it was simply not enough.

She went to see Mary, because she thought she alone might be able to persuade Stranragh to stop being so vindictive and foolish.

'Lady Mary will be down in a minute,' said Maria, distantly disapproving, because of course she knew all about the scandal, and was determined to show Georgiana that she knew.

Georgiana sat back against the cushions, all pale and stuffed with feathers, and sighed with pleasure. Coming back to her own world, however fleetingly, was just for the moment bliss. It all smelt so lovely, and looked so lovely. There were too many flowers everywhere –

unlike the South Sheen households which never displayed anything but pot plants, and then only poinsettias that had long ago forgotten how to turn red, or Christmas cacti that drooped miserably on window sills, or avocado plants grown tall and irrelevant in jars that were too small.

There was scent on the lamps, as there always was in Mary's house, and there were discreet signs of a busy and active social life. Invitations to drinks, invitations to arts balls, invitations to private views, invitations to embassies, and one to a masked ball.

They kissed the air in greeting, and then Georgiana sank back against the feathered cushions, clutching at the comfortable memories they brought back, and waited for Mary to conduct what they both knew was not going to be a very graceful minuet.

Mary was not in the mood to be charmed by Georgiana. In common with her mother the Countess, she enjoyed scandals to do with other people's families, but not her own. She did not recognise in Georgiana the young really rather beautiful girl who had arrived from the Shires to stay with her only four years ago. She saw only a grown woman with foolish ideas and foolish attitudes. Earlier in the day, at the hairdressers, she had even imagined that Georgiana had taken advantage of her, and felt almost bitter about it. She had taken Georgiana in, she had helped her achieve some sort of social life, when her own parents would have been quite happy to leave her to rot at Longborough. Of course she had had nothing from it, nothing at all except expense and now, scandal.

'You seem to make a habit of running off with the

most peculiar people, Georgiana. Forgive me for saying so, but it's true.'

Georgiana had noticed, of late, that people who begged for forgiveness rarely, if ever, deserved it, or indeed desired it. She looked at Mary with a new sense of sharpness. She was a beautiful woman with hard edges. She had style, of course, borrowed style, but she was not what Gus would call an 'original'. She was brilliant socially, never at a loss, utterly charming, and had always been asked everywhere, for she was an undoubted asset. Someone you could put next to anybody, because she was not quite somebody.

'Do you think I could have a coffee?' asked Georgiana.

'Very well.'

Mary rang for Maria, and Georgiana listened while her 'order' for coffee became a major diplomatic incident. There was no real coffee it seemed, only powdered coffee, and then only decaffeinated powdered coffee, because this afternoon was Maria's day for going to 'market'. (Mary always left off the 'super'. All part of the 'style'.)

'So.'

'So.'

They faced each other once more. Mary wondered if Georgiana was going to make a scene. She was quite prepared for it, and equally prepared not to give in to anything.

James was quite right to want his child back. He couldn't have him brought up in some ghastly slum by some depraved character that Georgiana had taken a fancy to. It would be terrible. People's upbringing influenced the rest of their lives. The future Baron Stranragh must be someone you could ask to dinner, and not feel embarrassed by.

'You are seeing James at the moment?'

'I have always "seen" James, Georgiana. What do you mean?'

'Of course. I mean you are in contact with him.'

'Yes.'

'So you could persuade him that George is not his child?'

'If you can persuade me, I can tell him.'

Georgiana looked away from Mary out towards the houses opposite.

'It's difficult to know where to begin.'

Mary said nothing. She fully expected not just a tissue of lies but a box full of tissues, but pluck at them as she would, she was not prepared to let Georgiana off this particular hook. She was a good fisherwoman and enjoyed a bit of sport, which, she felt, Georgiana was about to provide.

'I'm sorry about Hugo and Lucius,' said Georgiana suddenly.

Mary's composure dropped momentarily into the collar of her shawl-necked cashmere jumper. No-one except herself and James knew about Hugo and Lucius. She hadn't, yet, even told her mother.

'Life's so strange,' Georgiana went on. 'Even Italy is a very small place.'

She saw Mary's confusion, and if she had had a less kind nature, she would have enjoyed it. Not that she wouldn't have liked to, she thought, that there was no denying; but Mary was a middle-aged woman, and your lovers running off together, when you were older and had less chance of replacing them, was only amusing to your friends. If the quality of mercy had not been so alive within her, she would have told Mary the exact circumstances in which she had encountered Hugo and Lucius.

It had been at the end of the summer, moving into early autumn; *fin de saison* hung from every basket in every small square through which they passed. Gus had, most unusually, sold a picture. As with most of his sales, upon receipt of the cash he felt it his solemn duty to spend it. He decided to take Georgiana south to Calabria. Calabria in the autumn was full of a brooding atmosphere, unchanged since the earliest times. He felt it imperative that she should sample it before the tour operators destroyed it. Georgiana wished only to stay where she was, so naturally they went south. On the way, Gus forgot about Calabria's brooding presence and was suddenly reminded of how much he had loved Capri. Georgiana really only wanted to go home, so naturally they went to Capri. And it was sitting in the central square, gossiping together, that they had seen Hugo and Lucius strolling by in that intimately detached way that shouts 'affair' to the onlooker. They had greeted each other because there was nothing else they could do. From the manner of their exchanges, no-one could have guessed that Lucius had really rather loved Georgiana once. He had loved to buy her clothes, and she had been a willing victim of his good taste, but now he was in another world, a world he couldn't tell her about, so he no longer loved her but moved away, following Hugo towards a table which was well out of reach of memories.

'Yes, they've gone to Capri,' Mary admitted in a flat voice. 'They're renting my house. It's all very civilised.'

'Everyone always says that when it's not.'

Mary looked at Georgiana. It was obvious now that she was not going to make a scene. It was also obvious that she had changed. Not outwardly (although her clothes were a little peculiar) but inside where she had once been malleable Mary saw that she was not quite so any more. She felt trapped in a strange way, as if she had gone to a party expecting friends and found only people she didn't know, or perhaps didn't even want to know.

'You've changed,' she said.

'Yes, I suppose I have,' said Georgiana, and smiled suddenly. 'About time,' she said.

'It must be terrible for you, your parents disowning you, and now the baby—'

'I'm very happy,' Georgiana interrupted. 'And no-one can take the baby, because he's ours, not James's.'

'I think you'll have to let the lawyers decide that one. Ah. Coffee.'

Georgiana waited, formally, until Maria withdrew, even though she knew that she would stay outside the door to listen, as she always had done when Georgiana lived with Mary.

'Very well,' said Georgiana, 'if you think that's best, but it'll all be very expensive and silly, and it'll only mean that we'll have to bring George back from Italy.'

'He's in Italy, is he?'

'Yes,' said Georgiana, and smiled again.

Mary thought 'so that's why James's people can't find him,' and smiled back.

'I thought, you see, I thought you, because you're so sensible, could persuade James to call his men off. You know the trouble with neighbourhoods like ours, everyone notices when there's a sudden influx of "window cleaners", particularly since they all do their own.'

Mary didn't think she liked being sensible. In fact she was quite sure she didn't, and she certainly didn't like Georgiana's new 'tone' with her. It wasn't at all what she desired in a younger cousin. She wondered, fleetingly, if her new confidence sprang out of something else, but there was no doubt about it, her pupils looked normal, her hands didn't tremble, her complexion was fresh, and she looked well in every way.

'You can't blame James—'

Mary crossed her long elegant legs and stared at Georgiana with her odd eyes.

'No, I know,' said Georgiana. 'I am James's wife and I have had a baby, and I shouldn't have told him that I was pregnant when I wasn't, but then he shouldn't have beaten me up.'

There was a pause as Mary thought out how best to play this one, and then having decided, acted upon it.

'I don't blame him.'

Georgiana smiled.

'He beat me up because I wanted to leave him – you see,' Georgiana put her cup down, 'he's got sexual problems – well, apparently it's because of his dead mother. He keeps her portrait opposite his bed—'

'I don't want to hear any more,' said Mary sharply.

Georgiana remembered Mary's intolerance of anything remotely real. Pictures of dead mothers, Freudian

225

problems, they were not something she would care to discuss.

'He really needs to see a doctor.'

Mary looked at Georgiana. How she pitied her. She was making a fool of herself, and in a way that was going to be tragic. Roses round the cottage door and love's young dream lasted just so long, and then life became a morass, there was no other word for it, of ugliness and quarrelling.

'Gus is the father of the baby, Mary,' Georgiana was saying, 'really. If you could see him you'd understand.'

Mary couldn't wait for Georgiana to leave.

'I think it's best if you go now,' she said.

Georgiana let herself out of the house, pulling the much-morticed door shut behind her.

She waited patiently in the rain, sheltering with the other travellers under a shop front. She was sure that Mary would have telephoned James the moment she left the house, and that James would finally believe that the baby had gone to Italy, and that he would at last settle the whole matter by a blood test, and there would be an end to lawyers' letters and private detectives with chamois leathers creeping round South Sheen.

She climbed on board the bus, choosing, as she always had done as a child, to sit upon the seat for three, her legs swinging free. Old ladies with shopping bags climbed up beside her, and she sat confined but happy. She watched her familiar world receding now, as little by little the nature of the shops changed, and the clothes of the passers-by too. Now there were children playing in the street, dogs roaming and litter bins spilling with old cartons that had once held greasy chips. Old men waited with evening papers leaning against the bathroom-tiled pubs. Tired drays, blinkered against the traffic, pulled carts with empty casks home. It was an old world, with its rhythms and its realities. For her, London had once been the shallow mile around Harrods, but now it was over the river and into places that she had once loved to mock.

'Why?' she had once asked the Countess of the Duke of Windsor's love for Mrs Simpson.

'Love is blind,' she had said with impatience, and had turned away.

Putting her key into the lock of their front door, and looking up the small bare hall to where Gus was lounging in the kitchen with a mug of tea and his feet upon the fire guard, Georgiana had little trouble in believing her.

# 11

There was a small row brewing between Fulton and Elliott because Lady Tizzy had been discovered climbing in the dining room window. Fulton was all for putting his foot down and being firm, but Elliott was too afraid of her taking the kind of line that they both might regret and going off to the Bahamas with Victoria and Nanny. He thought he could *manage* Lady Tizzy in a better way, and defeat the horrible Ron without there being some sort of showdown where everyone ended up breaking the one thing of which they were fondest. Fulton had his doubts, which he articulated quietly and often. He did not like showdowns either, but he felt that now that Patti was being so blatant in her habits they were justified in having 'a word'.

'Out all night and asleep all day, she's worse than a cat,' he complained, but Elliott calmed him, and much against his will he was sent off to his auction after yet another talk, when what he really wanted was a blazing conflagration that would clear the air and his head.

Elliott baked a cake, which he always did when he had to face Lady Tizzy for and on behalf of Fulton. He baked a chocolate cake, spread marmalade in the middle, and then looked at his watch, waiting for Lady Tizzy to wake at her increasingly usual hour of half past three in the afternoon. Tea laid beautifully on a tray, he climbed the stairs to the hussy's room.

'Knock, knock, Lady Tizzy,' he called, 'it's Ely-ot.'

'Hi,' called Patti, 'push the door. It's open.'

Elliott pushed the door and then, stepping carefully over garments that he would really rather not identify, he snow-shoed his way through Patti's thick white bedroom carpet, carpet that had been bought and paid for, the hussy, by Uncles Fulton and Elliott.

Elliott pulled the curtains and turned round. The room was a set for a new operetta, *The Strumpet's Return*. A muddle of make-up upon the dressing table, eyelash curlers, mascara, false hairpieces, hairbrushes to straighten the curls that had been accomplished by an army of heated rollers of fiercesome shapes, lipsticks shot up from their cases lidless and helpless, some abandoned half-way, grotesquely shaped tops of nail varnish bottles whose contents were encrusted round their necks ('Orange Peach', 'Snow Pearl', their names belying their fearsome colours). And over everything hairpins, small, bent, large, pronged, metallic, and contorted without their owner's crowning glory.

'Oh, Patti?'

There was a groan from the bed, and from among the double downies and the lace Patti emerged pale, large-eyed, and with her greatest asset spilling generously over the top of her plunging mauve satin nightgown. It was a sight that would have stirred most males, Elliott realized, but at that very moment he was too preoccupied with trying to make some sense of the room, before the tea sat for too long and became undrinkable.

Patti yawned without putting her small white hand in front of her still reddened mouth. She didn't need to ask Elliott the time for she could tell from the fact that he had brought her up a tea tray and her favourite chocolate cake that it must be about four o'clock.

'I feel just like when I was a dancer,' she said, sitting up and plumping up her pillows. 'You know? We never used to get up till late afternoon if we could help it, it's a great feeling.'

'Really?' said Elliott, searching for a box into which to put the hairpins. Finding one, he then abandoned the clearing up and sat down to pour the tea.

'Thanks, Ely-ot.'

'Choccy cake?'

'No thanks.'

Elliott stiffened.

'What do you mean, no thanks?'

'I don't know,' said Patti, and she looked puzzled. 'I've gone off chocolate at the moment. But this *tea* is fantastic.'

'But this is your favourite.'

'I know it's my favourite, but I just don't fancy it, and I don't know why.'

'I'll have some, then maybe you will,' said Elliott, cutting it.

'No, really, I couldn't.'

Elliott cut his up and then popped it in, piece by piece. He savoured his own cooking, but not when the person for whom he had cooked wasn't sharing it with him. Masterpiece though it undoubtedly was, of both lightness and texture, not to mention subtlety of taste, it was ashes in his mouth as a solo experience. He couldn't drink alone, and he couldn't eat alone, but eat he must and look relaxed, for he had a mission to accomplish.

'Try a tiny bit.'

'All right.'

Patti tried a tiny bit. She chewed it dutifully, full of the cheerful willingness to please that made her such a difficult person to abandon, even when you knew you should, thought Elliott. She was a naughty puppy that should be smacked and yet somehow never was.

'Urgh—'

Patti put her hand to her chest dramatically.

'Out of the way,' she commanded.

And then she sprang out of bed and rushed off towards the bathroom. Elliott stared down at the cake. It tasted perfectly all right to him. The recipe was the same that he always used, lovely and squashy, and the Countess was always angling to know the exact ingredients, so what was happening? A ghastly thought came to him. Supposing something had fallen into the mixing bowl? Something unspeakable that people wrote about in restaurant guides?

'Are you all right?' he called out to Patti.

After a long pause that was filled with the unmistakeable sounds of retching, Patti emerged a beautiful eau de nil colour. It set off the mauve nightgown to perfection.

'Not a toe nail in the sponge?' asked Elliott tremulously.

'Don't be silly, pet.'

Patti climbed back into bed and lay against the pillows, a silent, waxen doll-person.

'I made it just as I always do,' said Elliott, lifting the sponge gingerly with a knife and peering into it.

'Don't be silly,' said Patti again, 'it's got nothing to do with the cake, it's me. Course, it makes such sense now.'

She ran her hands over her greatest asset with a swift movement that held more than a hint of the medical. Elliott looked away. It wasn't his sort of thing, really. And then he looked back.

'Oh, my God,' he said, 'you don't think you're—'

'That's just it, I do,' said Patti in a flat voice.

'I don't believe it,' said Elliott in an equally flat voice.

'Oh yes you do,' said Patti. Her eyes filled with tears. 'Just my luck.'

'Luck has very little to do with it,' said Elliott, springing up and moving away as if he was afraid he might catch something.

He walked up and down the bedroom a few times but then, finding it too tiring on account of the thickness of the carpet, he sat down again.

'What are we going to do?' he asked Patti.

'Nothing much we can do,' said Patti, still crying. 'It's done now.'

'What are we to tell Fulton? He'll have a fit.'

'*He'll* have a fit! He hasn't got to have the flaming thing,' said Patti.

'Last time he said he couldn't go through it all again.'

'*He* couldn't – oh dear, here we go again.'

As Patti rolled out of bed once more and swam blindly towards the bathroom, Elliott heard Fulton's white convertible Volkswagen with gold wheels pulling up.

They met in the drive. Fulton swung carefully out of

232

the car, smoothed the creases from behind his legs, and straightened up.

'What's the matter with you?' he asked Elliott.

'No-thing,' said Elliott, who had tried to fix his face in a casual expression, but obviously failed.

'One of the great things about you is you're such a rotten liar.'

'Drawing room?'

'Of course.'

Fulton followed Elliott into the drawing room. Elliott turned and faced him, one hand upon the chimneypiece, the other held tensely by his knee.

'You've had a blazing row, and she's leaving and taking the baby?'

'No,' said Elliott.

'Worse than that?'

'No, a little better, but not a great deal better.'

'Ron wants to marry her, and they want to adopt the baby?'

'No, not as bad as that.'

'I give up before I throw up.'

'You've put your finger on it, my friend.'

'Throwing up?'

'Precisely. She's *enceinte* once more. Can't even keep her favourite chocolate cake down.'

Fulton lowered himself suddenly on to his favourite Knoll sofa. He felt at once that he must have seen a single magpie and forgotten to say his invocation against evil. He felt that he had been walking happily along and someone had mugged him. Life had mugged him.

'Oh my God,' he said, which was the strongest term he ever used.

'He'll have to come to our rescue.'

He put his head in his hands. The idea of a little Gillott had been bad enough, but then that *crise* had been averted and everything had turned out beautifully, but now here they were faced with a little Ron. PC anything but Plantaganet.

'We'll just have to go and see her, and talk it over.'

She was still in the bathroom as they knocked and walked into the silent bedroom.

'Don't look,' whispered Elliott. 'I haven't tidied up yet. I've been in such a—'

The bathroom door opened and Patti emerged once more, still, Elliott noted, a beautiful eau de nil.

Fulton watched her climb into bed without any outward emotion. He felt sorry for her, terribly sorry for her, and he also wanted to strangle her. She had about as much sense as a farmyard cat, and just about the same lack of discretion.

'I hear you think you're *enceinte*?'

Patti looked at him through eyes of suffering.

'You'd feel old if you'd been as sick as what I've just been,' she said wearily.

'What he meant was—'

Fulton threw Elliott a look, which he caught, and there was a short pause in the proceedings while Patti groaned again. Elliott set himself to doing some more tidying up because he felt, quite rightly, that there was very little else he could do. He found himself counting the hairpins, and then stopped when he reached fifty-nine, because it wasn't making collecting them any more interesting.

'So,' said Fulton with composure, once the groaning had stopped, 'where, as they say, from here?'

'Down the plug hole,' said Patti.

'Yes, but besides that, where from here?'

'What do you mean?'

'You know very well what I mean. The future is in your hands.'

'Well I'm not doing anything about it, if that's what you mean. It's against my principles.'

'But you haven't got any.'

'No, I know, but if I did, it would be against them. I'll just have to go through with it, and there's an end to it.'

'You seem to have a – oh, well, never mind that now.' Fulton sighed.

'You can divorce me if you want,' said Patti, tears balancing on the spikes of her mascara, reminding Elliott of dew on a spider's web. 'I wouldn't blame you.'

'No, I wouldn't blame me either,' said Fulton with some force. 'It's not as if you take much interest in the one you've got.'

'There's not much point,' reasoned Patti, 'not with you two, and Nanny.'

'*She's* got a point there.'

Fulton threw Elliott another look, and he set about culling as many of the old lipsticks as he could lay his hands on.

'It has to be said, Patti,' said Fulton above the sound of the lipsticks being fired into the wastepaper basket, 'it has to be said that, as your husband, I feel I have the right to know who is the father of my next child. I do feel I have that right.'

'Course you do.' Patti sniffed. 'And I'll tell you.'

Elliott stared critically at the end of a lipstick,

wondering whether he should be ruthless to 'Passion Fruit' or whether he should spare it? He plumped for mercy, withdrew it into its mottled silver case, and finding its lid, placed it in the drawer of the dressing table. During this time Fulton had found Patti a handkerchief, and Patti had made use of it.

'See, you know I was mad about Ron? The policeman?'

'*Yes*,' they said together.

'Well he threw me over. Six weeks ago last Wednesday.'

Patti stared bitterly ahead of her.

'It wasn't as if we'd got anywhere anyway. I mean I think he just used me as a ticket to Screen One and Two, and free zings.'

'Zings?'

Fulton hesitated.

'Was that – something you did together?'

'No, it's a drink he likes. Anyway, it was all right, I mean I thought it was all right, until we came out Wednesday six weeks ago, and he said "Patti, much as I love you and our afternoons together, it's got to stop".'

'Oh well, at least he was clear about it.'

'Sure,' said Patti, 'he was clear about it.'

'So that was that?'

Patti turned to Elliott.

'Yes, that was that all right. The snob.'

'Thought he was a cut above you, did he?' asked Fulton, slightly surprised.

Patti unwrapped a piece of her favourite chewing gum and masticated it slowly.

'No,' she said through the gum, 'that wasn't what it

236

was. No, he dropped me 'cos he said he couldn't cope with me being a Lady.'

She sighed and looked wistful.

'I honestly never realised before what a strain it is being, you know, upper class and everything. But I do now.'

The silence held, just, and Elliott quickly resorted to examining the multitudinous nail varnishes again.

'So. If it's not Ron, who is it?' asked Fulton.

'Same as before,' said Patti briefly. 'We seem to have an irresistible urge every time we see each other.'

'That goes without saying,' said Fulton. 'Well, at least my children will be related.'

'Yes,' said Patti brightening, 'I never thought of that. That'll be nice, won't it?'

Fulton breathed in deeply, and then kissed the top of her tousled head.

'You just stay where you are,' said Elliott, 'and I'll bring you some clear broth in an hour or so.'

Patti lay back against her pillows and sighed.

'You know, you two are very good to me,' she said.

'We know,' said Fulton and Elliott together.

Downstairs they shut the drawing room door and faced each other once more, across the fireplace.

'Two will be rather nice,' said Fulton, once they had recovered their composure.

'Certainly,' said Elliott, 'particularly two girls.'

'Yes, matching taffeta frocks and little ballet shoes, and things.'

'Patti's not the type to have boys, is she?'

'Definitely not.'

'A nursery full of Melburys, what a to-do.'

'Yes, it's going to be lovely for us, I know that now,

but I think we ought to tell "Dad" that after this – that's it. I mean the school fees, Heathfield, Switzerland, it's going to bankrupt us.'

'Yes, but what fun.'

'Yes, I know,' said Fulton trying not to smile, 'it is, isn't it?'

'Champagne?'

'Naturally.'

'Sophia Emerald – Mapp.'

'No.'

'Oh very well, be stuffy.'

Fulton spread his hands out across the fireplace.

'We'll commission a portrait of them – "The Misses Montrose-Benedict-Cavanagh".'

But he spoke to an empty room, for Elliott had gone to fetch the champagne.


Jennifer, the official mother of the Marquis of Pemberton's official family, was busy preparing to receive the Countess for tea. She checked the dining room where it was laid. She enjoyed the new custom of tea rather than drinks, the eternal 'drinks', because she liked to think it was less harmful. Bloss did not enjoy it. In fact she quite thought from the way he banged her best Wedgwood cups down that he disapproved of it. It wasn't as if she asked him to make the cakes or anything, but even so, he put up with 'tea' with great ill grace. Jennifer was looking forward to seeing the Countess for one reason only, the same reason she felt that the Countess was looking forward to seeing her, so that they could discuss Georgiana and her fate in complete safety.

There was no doubt that they had become 'friends'

since the Countess had moved down to Wiltshire (if that's what you did from Sussex). Anyway, she thought, it was very nice for both of them, for both of them were, in their way, just a little isolated behind the façades of their houses, moving among their things, and no doubt enjoying them, but not finding their 'things' quite enough to satisfy.

'It's only really nice being alone,' said the Countess with precision, 'when you know lots of people want you. It's not nice being alone if you're not quite sure lots of people want you.'

'I'm afraid,' said Jennifer, passing her a small selection of sandwiches, 'I'm afraid, as you know, I have never been very much in demand.'

They both knew that the Countess knew that, and there was very little point in dissembling, so the Countess didn't. She stared instead at Jennifer. It had come as a surprise to her that she not only got on with this plain daughter of the former Mrs Parker-Jones, but actually liked her. She couldn't like her taste, of course, that would be impossible, but she found herself respecting her, and considering her mother, that was remarkable in itself. They were as one on the subject of Georgiana, and they were also as one on the subject of not discussing the subject with anyone else, least of all the former Mrs Parker-Jones.

'How was she?' asked the Countess, getting to the point just shortly after her sandwich.

'Do you know—' Jennifer paused, 'do you know she looks very well?'

'How was he?' The Countess chose another sandwich, sardine and lettuce, one of her favourites.

'He is very much a painter.'

'Yes, ghastly people, aren't they? Dubedats the lot of them.'

Jennifer nodded, even though she didn't understand to what the Countess was referring.

'Of course they'll starve. Her parents won't have anything to do with her. They've cut her off, Stranragh's cut her off, of course, and so that's it, isn't it?'

Jennifer sighed. It was all so peculiar, she thought, what with Georgiana always having been the beautiful one.

'She'll get bored of him quicker than he'll get bored of her. It always happens in those cases.'

The Countess spoke with the authority of someone who had always had an address book full of more names than the London Telephone Directory.

'I asked her down, but I don't think she'll come.'

'No, of course not, doesn't want to see you all happy and comfortable surrounded by your sons. Pemberton so devoted.'

'Yes, I must say he is devoted.'

The Countess nodded.

'Last week, he gave me a wonderful brooch, all diamonds and things. Quite lovely.'

The Countess smiled, and thought well he would, dear, wouldn't he?

It had always gone on, of course, the family being brought up at the Hall, the by-blows in the village. Nothing too terrible about that; so long as they didn't all fall in love with each other, everything would be all right.

'I thought we'd go over to the nursery after – after

we've finished. Nanny's having baby Victoria to tea with the boys. Such fun.'

'Yes,' said the Countess, and dropped her napkin on the floor, always a good trick when you found your gaze faltering. 'I thought I'd talk to you about my taking on Andrew,' she said, once she'd straightened up.

Jennifer poured herself another cup of tea. She had used to like Andrew a little more than she did now. Now she really didn't like him because he was always 'up' to something. Either in the stables with Pember, or with Bloss and Pember in the pantry. If the Countess took him on, it would mean that he would come even nearer than ever.

'I thought he was going to China with a party of people who knew all about porcelain?'

'He failed the vet.'

'No?'

'Yes,' said the Countess. 'I promised your mama, and goodness knows I've tried, but it was no good. He went to meet them all at some club or another, and that was all right, until he had ten too many and passed out in the dining room.'

'My mother's instituted proceedings, as you know.'

'He'll be better once he's divorced, people so often are. Not one of my better matches, I'm afraid.'

'No,' Jennifer agreed. 'But then no-one can live with my mother. She only really likes Kensington, and then only when it's empty.'

'The country hasn't suited her, I would agree. And yet you it does suit.'

'Yes,' said Jennifer, 'I really think it does.'

The Countess smiled at her with something

241

approaching affection. When all was said and done, she was a good girl. She probably knew all about Pemberton's little fling, but she had no doubt decided to countenance it, which was very sensible.

In the nursery the two nannies were busy playing together, while the children sat in a solemn row, their Marmite fingers in front of them.

'How charming, how charming,' said the Countess.

Jennifer smiled. She was very glad that there were other babies arriving in the village. Even if Lady Tizzy's was a little bit of a strange set-up, nevertheless it meant that Nanny had a friend, and the children would have friends, and it couldn't have worked out better. She had heard from the 'Village Voice' (Mrs Dupont) that there would be a new announcement from Lady Tizzy soon, although how Mrs Dupont knew was a mystery. Except, she thought, perhaps not quite *such* a mystery, now she remembered that she had caught her with her collecting box creeping round the kitchen door the other day. ('Oh, Lady Pemberton, *there* you are. I couldn't get an answer to the door, so I thought I'd scratch at the back.') No doubt Jennifer would be asked to be godmother to the forthcoming new announcement, and doubtless she would graciously accept.

The Countess could only tolerate nurseries for so long, and then they started to remind her of her own grim days isolated among the roofs of her parents' house. She took her leave, and Jennifer retired to her little sitting room with her tapestry. Soon her mother would be leaving Wiltshire, and life would become greatly tolerable again. No more flying visits accompanied by lectures on how to run her own staff. No more complaints about Andrew and his habits. Mrs Gillott would buy a house in her old neighbourhood, and Andrew could live with the Countess, which would give the Countess something to grumble about, always an essential when you are getting older.

Jennifer liked everything to be neat and orderly, and so it was turning out to be. She felt that somehow she had had an effect in making it so, although exactly what she couldn't say, but she definitely felt that she had been an unseen force. The moving finger of Wiltshire, the *eminence grise* that had helped to calm.

She rang the bell for Bloss. He came to her call, which was almost a shock, for most of the time he pretended not to hear and skulked about in his pantry, busying himself with things that were of less importance than he imagined.

'Bloss?'

'Yes, m'lady?'

'Bloss. Yes. Bloss.'

Jennifer frowned at her tapestry, and then looked up at him, once she had thought of something to ask him.

'Were there any telephone messages while we were at tea?'

'Yes, m'lady, one from your mother.'

'I'm to ring her back?'

'No, m'lady.'

'Oh?'

Bloss paused.

'Just a message. It seems she's changed her mind.'

Jennifer rubbed the imaginary furrow between her eyes. She did not approve of her mother gossiping with Bloss, it was undermining in some way.

'Changed her mind? About what has she changed her mind?'

'About Kensington, m'lady. She says it's become an Eastern Bazaar. She's staying in Wiltshire.'

'Is that all?'

For Jennifer it was too much.

'Yes, m'lady.'

Bloss smiled to himself as he closed the door. He had persuaded Mrs Gillott to stay in Wiltshire for the good of the Hall, for the good of his lordship, and for the good of Bloss himself. Without her mother to annoy her, without that necessary distraction, the Unholy Alliance (as he and his lordship liked to refer to it), the Unholy Alliance would be uncovered. So long as Mrs Gillott remained a thorn in the side of the Seventh Marchioness of Pemberton, they could all be as merry as grigs.

He paused for a second, wondering what a 'grig' was. And then he put on his pantry apron and hurried out to polish up his brand-new Skoda hatchback. With a bit of luck it wouldn't be long before he graduated to a Vauxhall Astra, but just for the moment, he was really quite content.

# 12

Georgiana's parents had died in a car crash. It was unfortunate, for they were both JPs and had crashed into a tree after a cocktail party. The police had been most understanding in the circumstances and, in view of their standing in the country, had refrained from releasing details of anything except the tree.

Georgiana buried them at Longborough. It was a rainy day, leaves fell, and Nanny was going blind. Mary came to the church, and stayed afterwards to help 'field' the mourners, and prevent Nanny from killing herself with scalding tea.

They walked round the house together after they had settled Nanny in front of the telly.

'What will happen to it now?' asked Mary, pulling on her gloves, although they were inside. She gazed up at the cracked plasterwork, the mess on the paint, and the piles of rubbish everywhere. It was a disgrace, and Georgiana's parents were as much responsible for the whole beastliness as the tenants.

Georgiana walked on ahead, saying nothing. Mary followed her. It had been completely re-decorated only a few years before, and yet now, with that lack of care or interest for historic buildings that so often accompanied a lust for fox hunting, now it had returned to its former state with no trouble at all.

'The roof's still all right,' said Georgiana with satisfaction.

'Yes, the roof's still all right,' agreed Mary, 'that at least is an asset.'

The books in the library had grey mould dappling them. There were no paintings to speak of, thought Mary, just the kind of thing for which small antique dealers in provincial towns overcharged: pastoral scenes with badly painted horses in the foreground. No ancestors left, for the parents, had, it seemed sent them all to the sales in a fit of pique when Georgiana had left Stranragh.

'Of course the trouble with this house,' said Mary, who read the property column of *The Times* each week with devotional regularity, 'the trouble with this house is that it is too big, and has too little land. It is, at the present time, exactly the sort of property for which no-one is searching.'

'Quite right,' said Georgiana, peering into the Aga ovens and then quickly shutting the doors as they revealed themselves to be housing meat tins with rotting dog food.

'Your parents spent all their money on improving hounds, didn't they?' asked Mary.

Georgiana did not reply to that. Mary knew very well where her parents had spent their money. It was a useless subject to discuss.

'I must bring Gus down to see what he thinks.'

Mary sniffed, and then sat carefully down on the one chair in the drawing room that she imagined was free from damp.

'They could never have put the heating on,' she said,

as she felt the cold cushion under her sending her clammy messages.

'No, they didn't believe in that sort of thing.'

'I don't believe in that sort of thing,' said Mary, 'but you can't let the damp take over. It's absurd.'

'No, quite.'

Mary stood up again, and sat on the arm of her chair.

'I know Charlie Somerville at Brevilles, he could help you. I'm sure he could if I explained. He sold Petherington last year. Remember? No, you probably don't.'

Georgiana remembered him, but she said nothing.

'He sold it with potential.'

Mary crossed her legs in front of her in an effort to keep warm. Now she looked at her, now everyone had gone, she realised that Georgiana was looking quite decorative. Her clothes were really quite nice. Quite new. An expensive suit, shoes that were definitely not cheap, and jewellery that was modern. She had obviously made an effort for her parents' funeral, she thought with approval, quite an effort by the looks of it.

'Why do you want to bring "Gus" down?' she asked, putting a peculiar emphasis on his name as if it was foreign.

'Well,' said Georgiana slowly, 'funnily enough he's rather good at sorting things out. He has a flair for architecture.'

'But the architecture isn't what matters here,' said Mary. 'You've got that, what you want is to find its potential.'

'That's what I mean. Gus is very good at that. He did all sorts of things to our house, and kept it in period.'

Since they both knew the house in question was

a nineteen-thirties semi-detached villa, this statement made Mary snort in a mildly unfeminine way.

'Hardly the same,' she said, 'hardly the same.'

'How do you like Scotland?' asked Georgiana suddenly.

'I love it,' said Mary. 'It suits my mood in the autumn wonderfully.'

'Don't like the flies, do you?' asked Georgiana.

'Don't really notice them. James always has so many people coming up to stay, Mrs Peebles and I hardly set a foot out of doors, what with one thing and another.'

'I was never allowed anyone to stay.'

'James has changed a great deal in the last few years,' said Mary with dignity. 'You wouldn't recognize him.'

Georgiana thought she might, but she was not someone who cared to press a point when it could be suppressed and enjoyed later, and at leisure. She found the idea of James and Mary 'married' pleasantly amusing. They must suit each other perfectly with their mutual distaste for the realities of love and their overriding obsession with saving money in order to spend it on something to their own social advantage. Thus, it would go without saying, they would guard the larder key against the slightest infringement by the staff, but import fresh flowers from London, if they thought them necessary. Staff food would be laid out with strict 'wartime' observances, but at Christmas they would be given presents generous enough to make them reconsider handing in their notices. They would entertain their friends on an equally strict 'cutlet for cutlet' basis, but they would not indulge them. They would drift in and out of each other's lives during the day, exchanging information, and yet they would leave each other's thoughts severely alone. They would plan gardens and alter houses in an *entente* which could be easily mistaken for domestic content, but which was in essence merely only an uneasy alliance, a marriage of convenience.

'How is your "marriage"?' asked Mary, quickly changing the subject from James. She pronounced 'marriage' in the same way that she pronounced 'Gus'.

'It's fine,' said Georgiana in a surprised tone, because it constantly surprised her that it was.

'Things must have been quite tough for you,' said Mary with relish.

'Yes, things have,' Georgiana agreed.

'Not much money, and that sort of thing.'

'No, not much money, and that sort of thing. But all better now.'

'Better?'

'Oh yes, quite better,' said Georgiana, with equal relish. 'As a matter of fact – well, you wouldn't know this, why should you? As a matter of fact, Gus is quite rich now.'

'Really.'

Mary got up and searched her handbag for her powder compact. Georgiana stopped, and now she too got up. She wasn't going to present details to Mary when she was powdering her nose. In fact, now she came to think of it, she wasn't sure she was going to tell her anything more at all. It was dull to someone who was rich, although not at all dull to someone like herself who had just gone through *not* being rich.

'So,' she said, skipping the middle bits because they

were certainly too sensational. 'So sweet of you to think of Charlie Somerville, whom I remember quite well, but we shan't be needing him.'

She pulled on her satisfyingly thick leather gloves, her mind already halfway down the motorway.

'Who will you use?'

Mary snapped her compact shut, and the powder mingled with the dust that spun in the rays of the autumn sun.

'We shan't use anyone,' said Georgiana, leaving the room. 'No-one, we're going to live here.'

It would not take long, she knew, for Mary to find out upon what turn of the wheel her new fortune lay, and then she would doubtless remark 'yes, but that's not *money*', for there was money and money to someone such as Mary. Nevertheless Georgiana now had enough for Longborough and its needs.

Life had not become easier after she had married Gus, as it had not been expected to do. It had become feckless in some ways, careless in others, merry, casual, but not easier. They had lived from day to day in an improvident manner, not unlike the Flopsy Bunnies. It had not been helped by Gus deciding to turn his back on representational painting. Georgiana found this a pity, because, personally, she only really liked paintings that reminded her of something in her everyday life. Thus, before her second marriage, she had liked paintings of horses and flowers and pretty ladies, and now she liked domestic interiors with children and dogs sitting at breakfast, and subjects of that nature.

Every now and then, to her amazement, Gus had found a buyer for his new work, and once a gallery far away in deepest Shropshire had given him a small exhibition, but otherwise demand for his new work had slowed down to a trickle. He knew Georgiana didn't like it, but it didn't trouble him. Then one day, for a birthday present, he painted her exactly the sort of card that he knew she would love. To him it was sentimental trash but to Georgiana it was easily the nicest painting he had ever done, so she took it to a man who showed it to a man, and before very long they wanted more. Gus painted more to please her, and before long he was selling more than he could paint. Syndication rights for 'The Lady With the Far Away Look', as Georgiana came to call her, were sold to America. Money became something to worry about, rather than to count.

'So you'll be moving back here?'

Mary stepped ahead of her out into the dusk.

'Yes, we'll be moving back here.'

'I always wondered, we all did, why you "did it", you know,' said Mary, referring to her marriage to Gus.

'Yes,' said Georgiana, 'I expect you did.' She couldn't see Mary's expression now, which was a pity. 'Quite simply – for the fun.'

'Fun?'

'Yes,' said Georgiana, walking off towards her car. 'I've had more fun in the last few years than you've ever had.'

Mary watched her car disappearing down the drive. As far as she was concerned, 'fun' was a private party with a silken tent on the lawn, a weekend in the country when the guests arrived by helicopter, lunch in a private box at the races. That was, quite officially, 'fun' in a way that living with a painter in some wretched little house couldn't possibly be. She made a note to ask Stranragh what Georgiana could possibly mean.

On the way home Georgiana stopped at a small gardening shop. It had old musty wooden floor boards, packets of seeds for cottage gardens, balls of faded green string, and trugs for sale. She bought one. Soon she would be stepping out on to the lawn at Longborough and placing her own cut flowers in it. She wondered whether Hobbs, the old gardener, was still about; if he wasn't, there was sure to be someone like him.

THE END

Meet Georgiana, poor, posh and very beautiful, and Jennifer, rich, middle-class and very fat. Both girls share a common purpose; to find a suitable husband that will enrich or ennoble them.

Follow the changing fortunes of these two wonderful characters and their eccentric contemporaries in **Charlotte Bingham's** sparkling romantic comedy series.

BELGRAVIA

COUNTRY LIFE

AT HOME

Published by Bantam Books

## In Sunshine Or In Shadow

Brougham is the stateliest of stately homes, but for Lady Artemis Deverill it proves a lonely, loveless place. Eleanor Milligan, born in downtown Boston, knows only poverty and a continuing battle against bullying brothers and a sadistic father.

When Artemis and Ellie meet on a liner sailing to Ireland, they become friends, and spend an idyllic time in County Cork. But with the arrival of handsome artist, Hugo Tanner, it seems as though nothing will be quite the same. For in the sunlit prewar summer, all three become emotionally entwined, with startling consequences that threaten to haunt them for the rest of their lives.

### Charlotte Bingham

# STARDUST

Elizabeth Laurence is astoundingly beautiful. So beautiful she has never known what it is to have even a plain day. Used to the admiration of all, it seems that she will always be in charge of her own destiny. A star from the first minute she appears on celluloid, her future is certain, until she is cast opposite Jerome Didier in a hit play. Staggeringly handsome and tipped to become the leading actor of his generation, Jerome would appear to be made for Elizabeth.

But Jerome has fallen in love with the tousle-haired and carefree Pippa Nicholls, who is neither conventionally beautiful nor an actress and, much to Elizabeth's fury, he marries her. All is set for them to live happily ever after until the playwright, Oscar Greene, creates a part for Elizabeth which she intuitively recognizes is based on the character of Pippa - and Jerome is tragically deceived by the duplicity of his art.

Set against the glamorous world of theatre in the 1950s, *Stardust* is full of sharp insight into the destructive power of beauty: the stars who possess it, and those who live in their starlight. In Elizabeth, Jerome and Pippa, Charlotte Bingham has created three unforgettable characters, and *Stardust* is the triumphant achievement of a novelist at the height of her storytelling powers.

## Charlotte Bingham

Available in Doubleday hardcover

## TO HEAR A NIGHTINGALE

**'A delightful novel pulsating with vitality and deeply felt emotions'** *Sunday Express*

Brought up in smalltown America, Cassie McGann's childhood is one of misery and rejection. Fleeing to New York she falls in love with handsome Irish racehorse trainer, Tyrone Rosse, and when he marries her and takes her back to his tumbledown mansion in Ireland, it looks as if she has found happiness at last.

Passionately in love as she is, Cassie finds the all-male world of horses and racing rather lonely. There is much for her to learn, not least about the man she has married. And when tragedy strikes, it seems that Cassie must once again face rejection and lose her hard-won security.

## THE BUSINESS

**'The ideal beach read'** *Homes and Gardens*

Meredith Browne came up the hard way, starting at the bottom as a child actress. Max Kassov has always had everything. Despite their different backgrounds the two are very alike, and a mutual attraction deepens into a passionate love affair. But Max betrays Meredith; a vicious betrayal that leaves her humiliated and determined to rise to even greater heights than he - if only to exact retribution ...

Set in the glittering world of showbusiness, *The Business* is a powerful tale of romance and sex, of money and corruption, and of brilliant talent used and abused.

### Charlotte Bingham

Available in Bantam paperback